I LOVE YOU MORE

JOSIE RIVIERA

INTRODUCTION

To keep up on newly released ebooks, paperbacks, Large Print Paperbacks, audiobooks, as well as exclusive sales, I invite you to sign up for Josie's Newsletter today.

As a thank you, I'll send you a Free PDF ... The Beauty Of ...

Josie's Newsletter

Did you know that according to a Yale University study, people who read books live longer?

COPYRIGHT

I LOVE YOU MORE
Copyright 2016
Josie Riviera

DEDICATION

This book is dedicated to all my wonderful readers who have supported me every inch of the way.
THANK YOU!

PRAISE AND AWARDS

USA TODAY bestselling author
**Top 10 Amazon Bestseller Multicultural
Romance**
Top 100 Amazon Bestseller Romance
**Top 100 Amazon Bestseller Contemporary
Fiction**

CHAPTER ONE

"You needed to get away from the cold and come to Charleston. After the cancer scare and your divorce ..."

Anastasia grimaced at what her friend, Jaclyn, was saying as they walked to Jaclyn's car after a quick lunch. She took a deep breath. "It was difficult leaving Soo-Min with my ex and his newest flame."

"I can't believe Justin actually married Eliza. She's one of his students and half his age."

Anastasia shrugged, hoping the gesture covered her sadness. Despite applying sunscreen, she adjusted the wide-brimmed straw hat to protect herself from the sun. Then she averted her face to hide her tears.

"Valentine's Day in Charleston means romance. February fourteenth will arrive in two weeks and the streets will be filled with love and chocolate-covered strawberries and horse-drawn carriages carrying good-looking men," Jaclyn said with a smile.

"Thanks for setting up a free lawyer consultation for me." Anastasia lifted her travel bag over her shoulder and couldn't help a grin at her friend's matchmaking attempts. She'd need a city over-flowing with fragrant red roses and Sea Salt caramels to distract her from her lack of romance back in Vermont. "You could hand out 'I Love Charleston' badges because you like it here so much."

"I love Carolina blue skies and cloudless days." Jaclyn shaded her eyes from the afternoon sun. "However, I think they're predicting rain for tonight."

"Then those good-looking men in their horse-drawn carriages will get drenched." Anastasia re-garded a flower shop window overflowing with candy-red roses. Her grin faded as she reflected on her morning. Feigning a polite smile she hadn't felt, she'd handed over her precious four-year-old daughter to the man she'd once assumed she'd be married to forever. Now she believed his parenting skills were inadequate.

Although the textbook family she'd always wanted was gone, her priority was her daughter, and her determination to give Soo-Min a picture-perfect life remained firm.

"Your ex acts as if he's the next Shakespeare, but beneath that tweed blazer—"

"Is the father of my little girl," Anastasia said.

"He's the adoptive father."

Anastasia felt her face heat as she met Jaclyn's pale-blue gaze. "Whether a child is natural or adopted, the child is yours to love. In fact, you love that child more."

"I'm sorry. You're right. I've always considered my adoptive parents to be my true parents."

Anastasia gave her friend a quick hug. "Apology accepted. If Soo-Min wasn't mixed up in Justin's mid-life crisis, I wouldn't care what he did or whom he married."

Jaclyn tucked a strand of auburn hair behind her multi-pierced ear. "The custody dispute won't be easy. Justin is a community college professor and you're ..."

"A cancer survivor? Yes, and stronger because of the ordeal." *And fortunate to be alive.* "Is your bungalow far from here?"

"The house is in an oceanfront community a few miles across the bridge."

Anastasia easily kept up with her friend's pace. "Aren't you a struggling travel agent?"

Jaclyn laughed. "Yes." She pointed to a metallic-red smart car parked illegally and ducked into the driver's seat. "Get in. Oh, and I probably should've told you sooner, but it's not mine."

"Don't tell me you stole the car."

Jaclyn shook her head. "Not the car. The ocean-front house, and I didn't steal that, either. You remember my older brother, Luciano, don't you?"

An unexpected ache settled in Anastasia's throat. There wasn't a woman on the planet who wouldn't remember Luciano.

CHAPTER TWO

*A*nastasia's ears burned remembering the embarrassing crush she'd had on Luciano when she was in her teens. He'd arrive home from his Ivy League college on long weekends all dark good looks and chiseled features and a different girl on each arm. His Italian name had only added to his broad-shouldered charisma. Anastasia had developed an obsession for him and had followed him around like a giddy schoolgirl. Which, in her defense, she had been. They'd spent many evenings on his back porch after his boxing matches, talking and joking, although she'd done most of the talking while he'd offered encouragement and good-natured jokes.

"What's he doing in Charleston?" Anastasia asked.

"He relocated his software company here because he wanted to be near family," Jaclyn said. "He'll be thirty-five on Valentine's Day. He didn't want to celebrate his birthday alone, although he'd never admit it."

"I'm surprised he never married."

Jaclyn turned the corner so quickly that Anastasia held tightly to her seat. "He did, but he lost his wife to lung cancer several years ago." Jaclyn stopped at the guard gate of an exclusive community and rolled down the window. "Jaclyn Donati," she said, then turned to Anastasia. "Fate and my adoptive parents must've been playing a joke on me. I'm the Irish girl with a strawberries and cream complexion and the last name Donati."

Anastasia smiled, then winced. Soo-Min was from South Korea, and she'd never look like either Anastasia nor Justin. Soo-Min was petite, her dark eyes perfect and slanted, her coal-black hair spiking wildly around her round face.

Anastasia pulled the car visor down and regarded her own pallid complexion, dotted with freckles, in the mirror. Gone were the days of slathering baby oil on her skin to achieve a golden-brown tan. She lifted her bangs to regard the small scar from the melanoma surgery on her forehead, then quickly pushed her bangs down to cover the scar.

"If you ever see a suspicious spot on your skin, call me," Dr. Leskin, her family doctor, had advised.

"In the meantime, stay out of the sun for the rest of your life." She glanced at the small mole near her wrist and pulled down the sleeve of her cardigan to cover it. That mole didn't count. She'd had it for years.

Jaclyn started down a long driveway lined with hedges to a private courtyard. She parked and pointed to an imposing three-level mansion resembling an Italian villa. "Here we are, complete with maids' quarters. Luciano won't be back for hours. He gets so caught up in work that I need to remind him to take a breath and relax. That's why he's letting me stay with him while my bungalow is being refurbished. I'm his personal guru, and he can concentrate on being the math genius."

Jaclyn opened the large wooden double doors, and Anastasia stepped into the marble foyer. She set down her travel bag in the airy, circular hallway and drew an admiring breath. The living room floor-to-ceiling bay window provided a spectacular view of the Atlantic Ocean.

"The designer called this an open floor concept." Jaclyn flicked on an overhead shimmering crystal chandelier. "After all his work and sacrificing, this house is Luciano's reward. He loves beautiful things."

A tall, handsome man stepped into the living room and gave a lazy smile. "Are you speaking for me again, Jaclyn?"

Luciano. Anastasia tried not to react although her heart raced faster. His charcoal-gray polo shirt fit snugly around his muscular arms, his dress pants fit as if tailor-made. He was so tall he could've been a basketball star. In fact, she remembered he'd been offered a basketball scholarship but had turned it down. He'd preferred lifting weights and training at the boxing gym.

A golden retriever, whose muzzle was entirely gray, trotted beside Luciano.

Jaclyn stooped to pet the dog. "This is Lady."

Anastasia bent and stroked the dog's head. "She's sweet."

"And this is my brother." Jaclyn regarded Luciano. "You were supposed to be working at your office building in town."

"The weather service is calling for a storm so I decided to work from home this afternoon." He arched a dark brow. "Do we have company?"

Jaclyn stood. "You remember Anastasia, my good friend from high school?"

"He wouldn't remember—" Anastasia began. The dog nuzzled against her legs, gentle and welcoming. She stroked Lady's oversized floppy ears.

"*Si*, of course I remember you." Luciano's dark eyes warmed, intelligent and assessing. His rich chocolate-brown hair needed combing. "My sister's right. I love beautiful things." His admiring glance assessed Anastasia boldly.

She smoothed her skirt and stepped back. His slight Italian accent would forever make her weak in the knees. His handsome face sported the aristocratic features she'd remembered, and his nose listed slightly to the right as a result of the break he'd suffered from a boxing match.

"You always knew how to compliment a woman, whether you meant it or not," she said.

She waited for his rejoinder and was greeted with a broad grin instead. "Somewhere inside, I must've inherited the old Italian ways."

"Mom was Italian, too," Jaclyn reminded him.

Slight lines creased his forehead. "I'm referring to my real mother, not my adoptive one."

"Your real mother is the woman who raised you," Jaclyn said.

Anastasia sighed a little too loudly. She didn't want to be in the middle of an adoption dispute. "Where do you want me to put my things?"

"Will she be staying here?" Luciano asked no one in particular.

"If I'm a bother, I'll stay elsewhere." Anastasia bristled. "I don't need you to entertain me."

"Then you have changed." He smiled and the creases on his forehead disappeared.

There it was, that relaxed demeanor, the bald needling. Yet, simmering just below the surface, she knew he succeeded in keeping his true feelings carefully restrained.

Jaclyn glared at him. "Umm, a little rude, big brother, don't you think? I told you this morning before you rushed off that Anastasia would be spending the week with us in Charleston. She's meeting with Sam regarding a family court dispute because of her recent divorce."

"I apologize. I've had a lot on my mind and must've been preoccupied. Old friends are always welcome in my home."

"Or I can stay in Mount Pleasant," Anastasia offered. "Aunt Irina and Uncle Filipp retired there a few years ago, and they're expecting me to visit this week. They never had children and don't receive much company. I'll call them later to let them know I arrived safely."

"My bungalow is near Mount Pleasant so you can visit them when you check out my home renovations," Jaclyn said. "You don't need a week listening to your aunt extol the virtues of your wonderful mother, when we all know it wasn't true."

"If you remember, Anastasia's mother worked at the same hydraulic factory that I did," Luciano said. "We once compared notes on how much we disliked the harsh environment and hazardous working conditions."

Anastasia swallowed. Her mother's long hours. Factory work. She shook her head and held up a hand. Her lonesome childhood was a time she'd chosen to forget.

"I'll probably leave Charleston earlier than I planned, anyway," she said.

She was missing Soo-Min already, and she'd only been gone from Vermont a few hours. Perhaps she could catch an evening flight back and convince Justin to allow her to take Soo-Min for the night. Her daughter had seemed feverish when Anastasia had dropped her off. A bedtime snack of whole grain crackers and clear juice would help her sleep better. She could meet with Sam later in the week, when Soo-Min was feeling better.

Anastasia picked up her bag, intending to head for the door.

Before she took two steps, Luciano reached her and lightly touched her arm. "Please stay."

That deep voice. Guarded, but oh-so-smooth. Up close, she noticed dark circles under his eyes.

"Okay." She nodded and offered a brief smile.

She was here. She might as well stay.

Jaclyn pointed to an arched circular staircase. "The guest bedroom is upstairs on the right."

"Good. That's settled. You're staying and I'll retreat to my office." Luciano dropped his hand. "My investors are flying in from Europe tomorrow morning for the annual board meeting."

. . .

*A*nastasia's bedroom was adjacent to a balcony overlooking the ocean. After she unpacked, she showered and chose a long, printed blue jersey sundress with matching sandals. The fabric hung loosely around her thin frame, reflecting the weight loss she'd suffered as a result of her cancer treatment. Dr. Leskin had assured her that muscle loss, exhaustion and lack of appetite was normal. She wore a maxi dress to cover the thick scar on her thigh from her excisional surgery. Pulling her shoulder length hair into a messy bun, she concealed the scar on her forehead with side-swept bangs.

She grabbed her phone, opened the sliding glass doors, and stepped onto the balcony. The sea air, tangy salt and seaweed, teased her nostrils. Stretching out her legs on the chaise lounge, she plugged her phone into the wall socket and punched in her ex-husband's number. Frowning, she scratched the small mole near her wrist. The mole had swollen.

Jaclyn knocked on the sliding glass doors. "I'm off to the market for fresh salmon and rosemary, and I'll pick up Liz. She and Sam are siblings and partners in their family's law firm. Luciano's offered to cook dinner because I think he's feeling guilty for his earlier rudeness. He needs a break from that software project, but he hopes to hit the Forbes list if he can convince the overseas investors to buy in. Can you believe there's a list for billionaires?"

Anastasia stopped in mid dial. "Luciano's a billionaire?"

Jaclyn shook her head. "Not yet, but give my ambitious brother time and he will be." She checked her watch. "It's four o'clock and I'll be back in two hours."

When the door closed, Anastasia slid off her sandals and redialed her ex.

Justin answered on the second ring. "How was your flight?"

"What a difference four hours makes," she said. "Ten inches of snow when I left Stowe and now I'm admiring the Atlantic Ocean." *Enough small talk.* "How's Soo-Min?"

"Eliza and Soo-Min are outside playing in the snow. Wait. Eliza just came in."

A loud kiss was heard through the phone line.

"Hello, Anastasia," Eliza said. "It's freezing here."

"Is Soo-Min outside by herself?"

"Yes. Don't worry, the yard is fenced in and I can see her from the window. She loves the snow, and we had the best snowball fight. I let her win, of course." Eliza giggled at her own remark.

Anastasia gripped the phone tighter. Eliza was the reason that Anastasia's marriage had failed. Although, if she were honest with herself, Eliza was the last of her ex's several affairs that had foretold an ended marriage years before.

"I told you this morning that Soo-Min felt feverish. She shouldn't be outside on such a cold day." Anastasia swallowed past the tightness in her throat.

"Don't be so uptight all the time." Eliza covered the mouthpiece of the phone for a moment and whispered something to Justin. "Can you call back? We're ordering Asian food."

"Asian food might upset her stomach. The pediatrician recommends chicken soup."

"We'll order egg drop soup," Eliza said. "It's Korean, and Soo-Min will like it."

Anastasia took a deep breath. Eliza's immaturity had shown itself in neglect for Soo-Min one too many times. Through family mediation after an initial dispute, Anastasia had agreed to amicable joint custody. Up until now she'd had no choice but to comply, but that agreement was soon to be modified. "FYI, egg drop soup is Chinese cuisine," she said.

"I'll make a note of it."

"I'll call back at six."

"Make it seven," Eliza said.

"Of course." Anastasia's voice choked as she hung up the phone. Wait. She pressed redial. She'd forgotten to tell Eliza that Soo-Min was allergic to eggs. Weren't there eggs in egg drop soup?

Firmly, she shook her head and let the cell phone slide to the balcony floor. Justin would accuse her of being a helicopter parent if she called back.

She collapsed on the chair, feeling broken. Just the thought of Soo-Min spending winter break with Justin and Eliza was bad enough. Physically leaving her daughter in their neglectful care was worse. A small sob escaped her and she put her head in her hands.

Sometimes she wanted to protect her daughter so much she could hardly breathe.

CHAPTER THREE

*L*uciano strode up the stairs to the second-floor guest bedroom. He entered and crossed Anastasia's room to the balcony. Then he stared at the beautiful woman curled up and asleep on a chaise lounge. "Wake up. It's raining and you're getting soaked."

Anastasia jerked to a sitting position and stared up at him. He'd forgotten she had the most exquisite eyes, deep-set and round, a piercing, smoky blue-gray.

"Sorry, I must've dozed." She rubbed her eyes and shrugged apologetically. "I'm so tired lately that I fall asleep during the day without warning." Her pale-blue sundress had ridden up her legs, revealing a shapely calf and a thick scar along her thigh. She sprang from the lounge chair and smoothed her wrinkled dress. The hair from a disheveled bun framed honey-brown wisps of curls around her face.

"We both have sleep disorders," he said. "I don't sleep at night from insomnia, and you have narcolepsy."

She pressed her lips together. "It's fatigue, not narcolepsy."

"My mistake." He gestured to the heavy rain saturating the beach. "Nothing like a restful vacation in a perfect climate to put things in perspective. At least, that's what my sister tells me."

"This isn't a vacation."

He rubbed his forehead. "Right. You're here on business. If you want a lawyer who'll win your case and wring the most money out of your ex, then Sam's the right person. Just ask him how many cases he's won and he'll talk for hours."

"I'm not seeking counsel for additional money." She stood straighter. "Sam's not ethical?"

Luciano hesitated and waved his hand as if it didn't matter. "He's supposed to be one of the best. He's certainly my sister's man of the hour."

An avalanche of sideways rain blew at them. He bent to retrieve her phone and unplugged it from the wall socket. Then he picked up her drenched leather sandals, handed them to her and grinned. "Let's go inside before we're electrocuted."

She grinned back at him. "You really get a charge out of your own humor."

"Clever response," he said. "Although you should've dissolved with laughter because my remark was funnier."

She reached for her phone. "What time is it?"

"Six o'clock."

"I need to call my ex at seven."

He frowned. "You have plenty of time."

"Jaclyn hasn't returned from the market?"

"Many people are getting off work and trying to drive over the bridge to the mainland, so traffic might be backed up." He closed the sliding door behind them and strode to her private bathroom. Returning, he handed her a plush towel. "Dry off your sandals before they're ruined. Your hair seems damp, too." He reached out a hand and patted her hair. "I like your hair pulled back."

A sociable pat. After all, she was an old friend.

"You're welcome to explore the house, as I'll be working on my project a couple of more hours," he added." I don't want to restrict you to only your bedroom while you're visiting me."

Brilliant, just brilliant. You haven't seen this woman in sixteen years and you're reverting to what you did back then. Shameless flirting.

She was always such a good sport. Even at sixteen, she'd had a freshness about her, an intelligence beyond her years, and he'd enjoyed their hours of endless bantering.

"Thanks for the towel." She dried off her hair

and glanced toward the balcony. "I've never seen the ocean before and wanted to walk on the beach later. I've heard that the sound of waves is therapeutic."

"It's supposed to pour all night." He gave a short nod at the rain pounding against the balcony doors. "Wait until morning for your therapy."

A rueful smile lit her eyes. "I've waited all my life. I suppose I can wait another day."

A few minutes later, she padded barefoot into the kitchen.

"There's a threat of a thunderstorm," Luciano called from where he sat in his favorite leather chair in the living room. He'd clicked the radio to a classical station, and a Mozart piano sonata played softly from the home theater system. The golden retriever sat on the floor with her head cuddled in Luciano's lap.

Anastasia stopped in mid-step. "Do you make it a habit of appearing and disappearing? I thought you were working in your office."

"I was. I am. The dog kept barking and I assumed she needed a walk outside. Then I was distracted because I enjoy watching rainstorms." He glanced at the dog. "Lady doesn't like them, but she'll go wherever I go."

Anastasia regarded the floor-to-ceiling bay window and low gray clouds beyond. "Storms used to frighten me. When I was younger, I hid in a closet so I wouldn't see the lightning."

"You're not hiding in a closet now."

"There's no lightning." She offered a playful grin. Her luminous eyes gleamed as she stepped into the living room. "I realized that sitting in a dark closet by myself was more frightening than the actual storm." She rubbed the back of her neck, her grin wavered. "Now I've learned how to confront my fears, at least this fear, anyway."

She set her phone on the coffee table, then patted the dog. "I need to call my ex at seven."

"So you've mentioned," Luciano said dryly. "And Jaclyn phoned again. I told her to notify me when she arrived at Liz's house and then to stay indoors and wait out the rainstorm."

Anastasia nodded in that thoughtful way of hers. She'd always been so pensive. And charming. And affectionate. His adoptive parents had described her as "a hugger," whereas he was "standoffish and didn't allow anyone too close."

It's called personal space and people should respect it.

He lifted the beer he'd been holding. "Can I get you something to drink?"

She pressed her lips together and shook her head. "I'll see what you have, thanks." She padded to a corner cabinet stocked with beer and juices. She poured herself a glass of purple grape juice, then stepped back into the living room. Willowy thin, she moved with effortless grace.

She situated herself on the sofa and slanted a smile to him. His gaze dropped to her juice glass, then drifted to her face for a long moment. He wasn't surprised that she'd become an alluring, strikingly beautiful woman. She'd been an effortless beauty in her teens with her glossy honey-brown hair falling to her waist in a ponytail. And she'd never worn a drop of makeup.

She picked up a buttery-soft, red leather journal on his coffee table. "This is beautiful."

"It's from Italy."

"May I peek inside?"

He shrugged nonchalantly. "Suit yourself, it's empty."

She leafed through the blank journal and stopped at the last page. "Almost empty," she corrected. "There are some tiny words written in ... Italian? *Che Sara Sara*. What does it mean?"

"Whatever will be, will be."

She nodded. "From the song. 'The future's not ours ...,'" she sang.

"Che Sara Sara." Luciano chimed in for the ending.

"Who's it from?"

"My mother. This journal is the only memento I have from her. She told me to write in it every day."

She set the journal on the coffee table. "You obviously disobeyed your mother."

"There was nothing to write. I was a small child, and it was a scary time for me. When I arrived in America my adoptive parents tried ..." He turned to the window. The ocean, driven by a violent wind, seemed to connect with a bleak, leaden sky. Thunder rumbled from the distance. As if taking her cue from the storm, the dog huddled in a spot beneath the coffee table. The weatherman interrupted Mozart to upgrade the thunderstorm to a tropical depression.

Luciano turned back to her and raised his beer. "A toast to healthy living, Anastasia. At least for you."

"When you trained for your boxing matches, you ate lean meat, drank gallons of water and ate very healthy."

He shrugged. "I'm not a boxer anymore."

She took a sip of grape juice. Her smile was strained. "In response to your toast, Dr. Leskin advised me not to drink alcohol, and I'm following his orders."

His brows rose. *Why was she seeing a doctor?* She didn't offer an explanation. He didn't ask. He wanted to, but he didn't. He didn't know her that well. He knew her too well.

She tucked her dress discreetly around her

model-perfect form, her gaze fixed on the ocean. "I imagine surfing the high waves would be fun."

"Surfing would certainly be an adventure." He leaned back in his chair. He'd always felt content when she was nearby. She exuded a cheerfulness he rarely felt.

"You were an excellent swimmer," he said. "I used to call you a mermaid."

She flicked him a glance and nodded. "College scouts from my dream university attended my last high school swim meet. They were offering a full scholarship."

He shifted. "I'd heard you waitressed after high school."

Her long black lashes swept up. "I'd worked to save for college. Then I studied to become a teacher because I love children." She avoided his gaze. "You'd graduated from Yale and had moved away by then."

He tapped his fingers together. "Were you ever offered that scholarship?"

But he knew. God help him, he already knew.

She shook her head. "My mother didn't arrive home on time to drive me to the swim meet that day. She said she was working, although she always said that. It doesn't matter anymore."

"It *does* matter." He wanted to cross the room and take her hands in his. He wanted to explain how he'd tried to take her mother's eighteen-hour shift at work that day so she could leave early, but their boss had taken a long smoke break. When the boss had returned, he'd refused Luciano's request.

"Congratulations on *your* success, though," Anastasia was saying. "I always thought of you as a Greek god who could accomplish anything."

He hesitated. "I'm not where I want to be yet. I'll let you know when I've arrived."

"I'd say you're already there. You definitely made the right choice pursuing math rather than boxing." She pointed to the wide screen television placed over the mantelpiece of the gas fireplace, then swept out her hand. "Now you own a three story ocean-front villa complete with maids' quarters."

"And no maids." He waved off the compliment. "I'm sure your place in Vermont is nice."

"It's quiet. If you remember, the town has fewer than five thousand people." She chewed her full lips, then smiled too quickly.

The weatherman interrupted Mozart again, this time to upgrade the storm to a tropical disturbance. As if on cue, a clap of thunder vibrated from the distance.

Luciano took a long pull of his beer. He should check to be sure that all the windows and doors were closed and rain wasn't getting inside. Instead, he leaned back in his chair and fingered the bottle, enjoying her presence.

"You really get a charge out of your own humor," she'd quipped. He smiled inwardly.

"Now all you need to complete your magnificent villa is an oversized crystal vase brimming with candy-red roses," she was saying. "I saw a wonderful display today in one of the shop windows in town."

"Do you like roses?"

Their gazes met and her eyes welled with tears. "All women like roses."

He hadn't expected her to cry because they were discussing roses. He set down his beer and looked away. He didn't deal well with weepy women.

"Our lives are made up of different chapters," he offered. Adeptly, he'd changed the subject.

She lifted a well-shaped brow.

"You seem to be in the middle of a rough one," he added solemnly.

"Very rough, actually." Thick black lashes framed her beautiful eyes. Her cheekbones were high, her porcelain skin had a dream-like quality. He'd always found her stunning and had been amused, then flattered, when he'd realized she'd had a crush on him when she was in her teens. She'd trailed him everywhere, laughing at his sardonic jokes, the banter between them refreshingly exhilarating. She'd always 'gotten' his humor; their personalities had connected.

However, she'd been a high school sophomore

while he was a college sophomore. And he wouldn't permit himself to take the relationship any further.

Now he was a grown man and she was a grown woman, and his pulse stirred as he took in her perfect profile. Small, turned-up nose, and pale cheeks contrasted with the smokiness of her eyes. He'd never seen her that pale. She'd always sported a glowing-bronze tan because she'd spent hours in the pool during the summer. That span of freckles, which she'd always hated, was ever present on her cheeks, but now there was a slight scar along her hairline.

He rested his elbows on his knees and leaned forward. "Have you been ill?" Inwardly, he shook his head. He shouldn't have asked. *Too intrusive*.

But he knew her well.

He'd also learned to distance himself from others, especially sick others. The reflexive denial that a loved one could get sick and he couldn't do anything about it forever haunted him. He couldn't bear the thought of losing anyone else.

Anastasia granted him an amused look. "Luciano, where is your well-honed charisma? To ask a woman if she's been ill isn't flattering."

"I remember you as a vivacious, optimistic young woman with flushed cheeks who was never farther than a few feet away from me."

He expected her to smile, but her face remained impassive. "I experienced a cancer scare recently that ended up being melanoma in the early stages, and, thankfully, it was treatable."

"Perhaps you spent too many hours in the sun when you were a teenager. Your freckles used to turn red and burn."

Her eyes widened to defiance. "Do you think I'm some kind of idiot and should've known better?" She shook her head. "I remember when someone would get sick, you'd disappear from the room."

He returned her gaze and eyed her heated features. "Blame it on memories of an Italian hospital where I was forced to sit on a hard plastic chair and wait for news about my sick mother. I tried not to breathe in because the smell of urine and brown disinfectants was so strong I gagged. I waited hours before I was told she'd died the night before. Ever since, I've never liked feeling powerless."

His wife had also died unexpectedly. And there had been nothing he'd been able to do to prevent her death.

He sighed heavily, shrugged, then said aloud, "So there's your answer."

"I'm sorry," she said quietly. "I didn't know about your birth mother."

"No one else knows, not even Jaclyn." He motioned to the window. Tumultuous waves slammed the shoreline. "This storm has put me in a pensive mood. You were such a good friend and really listened to me when we were younger. Thanks for listening again."

"Perhaps this feeling of powerlessness is a fear you need to overcome, the way I overcame my fear of storms," she said.

"Perhaps." He gave her a meaningful look. "But you were a tanning goddess."

"Oh, for heaven's sake." She jerked to her feet. "I trained in the pool to shave seconds off my swimming times."

"I don't mean to offend you. In fact, I applaud your diligence."

"I see." She plunked her hands on her hips. "I was fifteen years old. Next time I'll know better and apply sunscreen." She went for her juice glass on the coffee table. It slipped from her grasp and spilled to the floor and the grape blush stained his pearl-white carpet.

"I'm sorry." She bent to pick up the glass. "I'll clean the mess."

"I'll hire a professional carpet cleaner tomorrow."

"No, I'll try to clean it," she said.

He raised a hand dismissively. "Don't bother."

She glared at him. "You know best." She grabbed her phone and whirled from the room.

CHAPTER FOUR

She hadn't reached the kitchen when thunder and lightning sizzled together. The brightest light she'd ever seen flashed from the living room window, followed by a loud bang. Lady panted noisily. Luciano knelt on the plush carpet, whispering softly to the dog.

The house went dark.

Somewhere in the house, fire alarms shrieked. Anastasia sniffed. The air smelled odd.

She dropped her cell phone on the counter and raced into the living room.

"There's smoke coming from the hallway!" Luciano shouted. He bolted from the living room and Anastasia followed closely at his heels. As they raced into his office, sparks jumped from a laptop computer sitting on a richly carved mahogany desk.

He grabbed a wet towel from an adjacent bathroom to smother the flame, then shook his computer and attempted to restart it. The computer didn't respond.

He brought a shaky hand to his forehead. "All my work," he mumbled.

She raised her eyebrows. "You didn't back up your computer files? Jaclyn mentioned you were working on some important project for weeks."

"Months."

Wind rattled the windows. He stared outside and didn't answer. The seconds ticked by before he turned to her. "My computer was connected to a power surger, but I didn't anticipate the house being struck by lightning. The weather service merely predicted a fast-moving thunderstorm."

"That was upgraded to a tropical disturbance, remember?" She whirled around. "I'd better get my cell phone." She rushed into the living room, attempting to switch on several lamps with a click. The air was flooded with the odor of charred wires. The sixty-inch-wide screen television whirred strangely, then blacked out.

Another bolt of ear-splitting lightning connected with the ocean. She raced to the kitchen, grabbed her cell phone and punched in Justin's number.

Luciano entered the living room holding his laptop. Lady whined beneath the coffee table.

Anastasia stared at the blank screen of her cell

phone and set it on the counter as a cold shudder went through her. "The phone's dead."

"The cell towers must've been knocked out by the lightning." Luciano pulled on a canvas field jacket and slid open glass doors leading to the out-door deck. "I'll check if there's any outside damage."

"I'll go with you."

"Okay. Leave the dog inside."

She scurried upstairs to her bedroom and grabbed a long cream-colored cardigan sweater and canvas slip-on shoes. She raced downstairs and slid the door shut behind her.

Luciano's lavish concrete deck sported a danger-ously overflowing hot tub and magnificent concrete urns filled with drenched flowers. Storm sirens wailed, adding to the chaos of dogs barking and ear-piercing fire alarms. Weighty rain pelted her cheeks. Shivering, she rubbed her arms and glanced toward the sand.

Something was happening to the shoreline, as if the waves sought to engulf every expensive home lining the ocean. A wind-borne sign crashed into a neighbor's gazebo.

A strange whoosh, whoosh filled the air.

Luciano assessed the sky and grabbed her hand. "This community hasn't experienced coastal flooding in years, and there's no time to board the windows. I'll leash the dog. We're getting off this island."

Her stomach roiled. With cold fingers, she touched his arm. "My purse. All my belongings—"

"Anastasia, the wind is picking up. I have things I want to save, too, but there's no time. Soon we'll be in the middle of a hurricane, and your cell phone will be the least of your concerns." He dropped her hand, slid open the glass door and quickly leashed the dog.

Lightning splintered through ominous black clouds, followed by a rolling boom. The roar of the wind shook the house.

"What's happening?" Icy panic strangled her voice. She felt chilled. She was sweating. She needed to talk with Soo-Min, her precious child. There was so much to say. If anything happened, she'd never have the opportunity.

Luciano returned within seconds and squeezed her hand. "I'll keep you safe," he said in a disturbingly calm tone. "You can call your ex when we reach the mainland."

"It'll only take a few seconds to run back into your house and—" She yanked from his grip, whirled and slipped on the loose sand blowing across the deck, twisting her ankle, landing squarely on the concrete. Pain and nausea rushed through her.

Holding the dog's leash with one hand, Luciano bent and smoothed a strand of hair from her face, his gesture gentle and unexpected. "*Mia Cara*, are you all right?"

Mia Cara. My Dear. My Darling. He'd never called her that before. She looked up into his strong features, at the man she'd cherished when she was fifteen.

She suppressed a moan of pain. "I'm all right. It's just a sprain." Her dress had ridden up and she glanced down at the ugly scar on her thigh, prominent and bleeding.

He pulled a wet handkerchief from his pocket and dabbed at her scar, then ran his fingers over her ankle, his dark head bent over her. "Nothing seems broken." He looked up and gave a reassuring grin. "Welcome to sunny Charleston."

She returned a slight smile. Somewhere nearby a tree cracked in two. She could hardly see three feet in front of her because of the heavy rain and wind, and he'd made her smile.

He covered her cold hand in his warm one and pressed it against his chest. "Can you walk?"

She nodded. "I think so."

"Or I can carry you."

"I don't need any help." She stood too quickly. A surge of pain in her ankle forced her to collapse against him. She attempted to pull away, but his arms tightened. He watched her, apparently waiting for permission to lift her.

"What about the dog?" she asked. "You can't carry us both."

"I lifted weights all those years just for this moment. I can carry you with one arm and lead Lady with the other."

Anastasia attempted to put weight on her ankle, bit back a groan and leaned against him. Seawater sprayed against her back and saturated them both. "I'll take you up on your offer."

"Good decision."

She gripped his shoulders as he scooped her into his arms. The storm shuddered as he sprinted to the side of the house where his Hummer was parked. He settled her into the passenger seat, clicked the seat belt around her, then unleashed Lady. The dog bounded into the back seat. Luciano belted the dog into a harness and tossed the leash on the floor.

"I'll start the Hummer after I check the road for potholes." He withdrew car keys from his pocket, then walked across the road, bending to check the depth of the rising muddy water. Muffled sirens sounded in the distance, although the island seemed deserted.

She rolled down the window and shouted, "Why is no one around?"

"February is the month to cruise the Caribbean, apparently." He turned back to the Hummer. Then he stilled, standing in knee-deep rushing water, staring at something behind her. He whispered something in Italian, then looked away.

Anastasia jerked around and met Lady's deep brown eyes, wide and panicked. She petted the dog's oversized paws, offering reassurances she didn't feel. When her gaze moved to Luciano's house, her breath stopped. One of the cement urns had become a twisted projectile and had crashed into the sliding doors. The terrifying sound of shattered glass filled the air, noisy and violent.

The wind twisted. Several hundreds of yards away on an empty stretch of beach, the force of ocean waves exploded the detached garage of Luciano's neighbor. Blowing faster, the wind lifted several roof shingles off Luciano's house. She blinked several times. *Impossible.* The roof was failing, the walls were collapsing. The hurricane was destroying Luciano's prized villa, carrying all his treasures away piece by piece.

CHAPTER FIVE

*L*uciano drove slowly through the flowing force of water, muscling the Hummer into the middle of the road, slipping the clutch and revving the engine. The wheels seemed to float.

"Open the door," he instructed.

"Why?" Anastasia's eyes widened. "We're trying to escape from the water."

"Trust me." He expelled his breath in frustration. "Letting the water flow into the Hummer will weigh it down."

Water poured in as soon as she opened the door.

"Now close the door. You can feel the tires gripping the road." He offered a reassuring smile and slipped one arm around her shoulder for a quick hug. "How's your ankle?"

"Much better."

"Once we're off this street, we'll be on the main road and take the bridge to Charleston."

She clasped her hands together and kept her gaze glued to the road. "Suppose the bridge is washed out and we're stranded?"

He couldn't trust himself to answer for the same thought had crossed his mind, although he wouldn't share that frightening possibility because it'd only worry her. He touched the brake lightly. The Hummer stopped.

He put the Hummer in neutral and attempted to restart. "The engine is flooded."

"What should we do?" she whispered.

He shook his head, more at himself than in answer to her question. As he stared through the windshield at the ensuing nightmare, he considered their options. None were promising. They could remain in the car or attempt to seek shelter in a building that might collapse on top of them.

Sweat dampened the back of his neck. Debris was wind-borne: garbage cans, market umbrellas, wicker chairs. Nothing and no one was safe from the torrential wind and incessant rain. He opened the door to assess the floodwater, and lightning lit the sky. Lady yanked from the harness and leapt out.

Luciano growled a curse and tore off his jacket. "Stay here. I'll go after the dog. The lightning must've terrified her." He grabbed the dog's leash, shoved himself from the seat and dove for the dog.

Lady was swimming against the current toward the ocean, her head above the chop.

He waded toward the dog, then hesitated. His grip tightened on the leash until his knuckles whitened. The water was getting too deep.

He fired a curse at himself.

Behind him, the door slammed. A movement in his peripheral vision caught his eye and an uprooted tree trunk plowed directly into him. Anastasia screamed.

His body flew forward into fast-moving water and he let go of the leash. His side throbbed. He slowly regained his balance, touching a hand to his side, wiping the stickiness of blood from his soaked shirt.

He should've been prepared for these types of storms. He'd bought a home on the ocean and hadn't even backed up his computer files.

Somehow, Anastasia had limped quickly to his side and was lifting his shirt.

"Get back in!" he shouted.

Her hands stilled. "You can't catch Lady on your own." Her lips pursed, her gaze met his long enough for him to see the terror in her eyes. She cut past him and retrieved the leash from the floodwater, then cupped her hands to her mouth.

"Lady! We're here, girl!"

Luciano swiveled, intending to go after the dog, and lost his balance. He plunged into the water a second time. Time slowed to pounding rain and one loud heartbeat after another. Anastasia's panicked cries resounded in his brain as he hauled himself to his feet. She reached him within seconds. Soothingly, she touched his forehead, and her tormented blue-gray eyes locked on his.

"Are you okay?" she asked. "You keep falling and I can't always save you."

He mustered a half-smile, coughed and tried to pull his thoughts together. "I couldn't be better." He shook away the feeling of lightheadedness and felt his body sway.

She turned toward the ocean and screamed a warning. A rumbling wall of white seawater surged, seeming to eat her words. He followed her alarmed gaze and a chill went up his neck. His beloved dog was swimming toward a stretch of downed power lines. The gale wind was moving over the ocean carrying a dome of water with it toward land.

Anastasia held up the leash and shouted into the storm, "Lady, come back!"

His chest tightened. Lady wouldn't be able to hear Anastasia from that distance, and they wouldn't be able to reach the dog because she was nearing the ocean.

No, please no! Don't let me choose because I won't make it. He shook his head, knowing it was his duty to save his dog. Sure, he was scared, but he wouldn't admit defeat.

He took one heaving breath and headed toward the ocean.

"Lady, come back!" Anastasia shouted again.

Miraculously, the dog turned and paddled toward them, managing the currents with inborn ease.

Anastasia turned to Luciano. She raised her freckled arms, ready to dive into the water. "Lady will tire soon. Let's meet her halfway."

Luciano eyed the distance. "The dog seems to be out of danger. You go. I'll wait here." He grabbed the leash from her hands.

"C'mon, we'll go together. Lady will think it's an adventure."

Luciano drew a difficult breath and stared down at the floodwater lapping at his thighs. "I can't ... swim."

She dropped her arms and repeatedly shook her head. "You bought a home on the ocean and you can't swim? How did you plan on reaching Lady a minute go?"

He flinched. "Fear primed my body, not my brain."

Her expression softened. "You're very brave."

"Or very foolish."

She wiped droplets of rain from her face. "I'll get your dog, and you get us back to the Hummer. Deal?"

"Deal. My Hummer can plow through anything." *If it starts.*

Without glancing back, she dove into the water.

He willed himself to wade deeper, but his feet remained planted firmly in place. He hated the feeling of being powerless.

Anastasia reached Lady in several strokes, urging the dog to paddle, navigating them back. He'd forgotten her championship swimming style, her lean, perfect form. She was ever-confident in the water, her strokes fluid and sure.

She stooped over and gasped for breath when she reached him. He laid one hand on her shoulder to steady her while he leashed the dog with the other. When Anastasia stood, shivering, his arm went around her waist. Personal space didn't matter anymore.

He thought she'd shove him away, but she drew nearer.

He gathered her even closer. "I'm proud of you."

She grinned teasingly. "All that swimming was just for this moment," she echoed his earlier words. Guardedly, he scanned her beautiful face for a sign that she thought less of him.

Her blue eyes twinkled, answering his question. "You'll always remind me of a Greek god, just a non-swimming one."

"I lived in an orphanage, not a beach resort," he said with a wry, self-depreciating grin. He kissed her cheeks with a soft brush of his lips. "Notice anything different?"

Her brows came together. "You sprouted gills?"

He laughed out loud. "The rain and the wind are lessening." Leaning down, he kissed her, one more time. "Thank you for saving my dog."

She placed a trembling hand on his cheek. "It's the least I can do for an old friend."

He glanced at the sky. A slice of sunlight shone through the clouds. "Let's go back." He kept one arm around her waist, the other firmly holding the dog's leash as they slogged through knee-deep flood-water to where the Hummer had been parked.

A makeshift garage floated by. Some of the smaller buildings on the island had been turned into toothpicks. She ventured a glance up and down the deserted street. "Your Hummer ... disappeared?"

He fixed his gaze on the empty road.

The air grew still. His arm fell away as he turned to search the shoreline, just in time to see his five-thousand-pound Hummer being swept into the ocean.

CHAPTER SIX

*T*hirty minutes had passed, and dusk descended at an alarming pace. Anastasia's sundress was dripping wet and she shivered, feeling cold and clammy. She threaded her hand through her hair, a soaked mass of tangles. Her gaze took in the devastation as they walked. The aftermath of the storm was as horrific as the storm itself. Sewer pipes were visible alongside downed telephone poles, and many luxurious homes were destroyed beyond repair. Strange, because some homes looked relatively untouched.

Her limbs felt heavier with each footstep, and her breath came slow and uneven. Her stomach growled, although she was more thirsty than hungry. She hadn't eaten since lunch.

Luciano offered numerous encouraging smiles

that he'd obviously perfected and slid a hand under her elbow. "We're nearing the main road," he said.

Sure they were. He'd said that countless times. She couldn't meet his eyes, couldn't force a nod, trying to shake the dregs of exhaustion. Perhaps they could sink into the soaking wet grass and sit quietly. The world had gone mad. It could wait a few moments while they rested.

The dog stopped abruptly, stared straight ahead and barked.

"Anastasia! Luciano! I'm so relieved I found you!" a woman shouted.

Jaclyn's voice.

Anastasia's head jerked up as she spotted a bright yellow canoe paddling toward them. She covered her mouth as tears welled in her eyes. Her thoughts jumbled and she leaned on Luciano, his arm secure around her shoulders.

Jaclyn. Here. It couldn't be.

But Luciano was waving, greeting his sister with a string of relieved curses.

Jaclyn slewed through the flooded streets like a pro. "Are you okay?"

"Yes, yes!" Anastasia's throat was thick. She broke free from Luciano and raced through the floodwater. She'd never been so happy to hear her friend's voice in her entire life.

Finally, she'd be able to call Soo-Min. She needed to talk to her daughter, to reassure herself that the world was still spinning. She needed to hold her. She missed her so much.

Jaclyn slid the canoe near them. "Get in so we can get out of here."

Luciano lifted a brow. "Don't tell me you stole the canoe."

"Nope, just the paddles," Jaclyn said. "Why does everyone think I steal things? That one time ... that one pair of earrings when I was a teenager that I didn't need anyway "

"That incident is water over the bridge." Luciano looked toward Anastasia for smiling approval of his joke, and she graciously complied. Then he planted his foot in the canoe's center, settling Anastasia and the golden retriever in the middle. Apparently mindful of the canoe tipping, he swung his other leg over, then sat at the other end opposite Jaclyn.

Jaclyn threw him a paddle. "First I needed a canoe rack. Then I needed two people to help me hoist the canoe onto the roof of my car, then I drove through really scary floodwaters. Consider all this a repayment for allowing me to stay in your house indefinitely."

He uttered a soft curse, his favorite epithet. "You said you were staying only until your bungalow was remodeled to your liking."

"I'm a perfectionist like you, and I'm not happy with the way the remodel is progressing. I'm adaptable, though, and I'll live in whatever million-dollar house you purchase next," Jaclyn said with a grin.

An hour later, the sky changed from dusk to darkness. They'd arrived at the bridge where Jaclyn ditched the canoe, then drove them in her smart car to her bungalow in a tidy residential area.

After everyone had remarked about the solitary toilet stationed in Jaclyn's foyer, they dried and changed. A few minutes afterward, Luciano lit a fire in the fireplace, then Anastasia and Luciano sat side by side on the living room couch.

Jaclyn had lent Anastasia a pair of lounge pants and a snug tunic top, and Luciano had changed into a spare tee shirt and jeans he'd kept in Jaclyn's closet. Several candles furnished flickering lights, and a battery-powered radio dispensed weather information. With a contented yawn, Lady found a comfortable corner by the hearth.

Soo-Min. Anastasia thought of little else, although she tried to concentrate on the conversation.

"I was driving to Liz's house when we lost phone connection," Jaclyn explained. "Who expected a hurricane to develop so fast?" She turned to Luciano, her tone tinged with amusement. "We penniless peasants weren't hit nearly as hard as you fancy island billionaires. Sorry you lost your villa, big brother. I know it meant a lot to you."

His expression turned impassive. "I didn't need an eight-thousand-square-foot home. I'll buy something smaller. Considering my lack of swimming abilities, perhaps I'm better suited to a place in the mountains," he finished with an apologetic shrug toward Anastasia.

She chuckled. "I can't box and you can't swim, so we're even."

"As long as your next mansion offers ample bedrooms and private baths, I'm good. " Jaclyn teased with a laugh. "Spectacular mountain views will be a nice change."

"I'll look for a house surrounded by acres of land at the top of a mountain." He gazed at Anastasia and wrapped one arm around her. A light came into his gaze, that powerful, unleashed determination. Nothing could stop him from reaching his goals.

She leaned into his comforting, masculine body. Despite her protests that her ankle wasn't swelled, he'd insisted on propping her leg up with several pillows and wrapping her ankle in a bag of ice.

She looked around. "Is there a cell phone working anywhere?"

"All the cell towers are down. Perhaps your aunt and uncle have a landline?" Jaclyn asked.

"Can you drive me to their townhouse? You'd mentioned they didn't live far from you, and I want to be sure they're safe. I'll make my call from there."

"Despite our ordeal, you're focusing on a phone call to your ex." Although Luciano shook his head in admonishment, his gaze held a gleam as if he were anticipating an enjoyable verbal sparring match to follow. "It's well past seven o'clock, so you missed *that* deadline. Does your ex know about your meeting with Sam, the lawyer extraordinaire?"

"I'm not meeting with Sam because of my divorce," she explained. "It's a free consultation regarding my daughter's custody dispute."

Luciano dropped his arm. "You have a daughter?"

She flashed him a smile. "Yes, she's four years old and in preschool." She reached for her purse to show him a picture, then realized she didn't have a purse, or money, or credit cards. Everything she'd brought to Charleston had been lost in the hurricane.

She drew a long, quavering breath. "All Soo-Min's precious baby pictures in my wallet are gone." Shock was wearing off and reality was taking a firm hold.

"Anastasia adopted her daughter from South Korea," Jaclyn was saying. "You probably were immersed in some business deal, big brother, and weren't listening when I told you a few years ago." She swiveled to Anastasia. "He always wanted a large family. As I mentioned, his wife died."

Anastasia placed her hand on his sleeve. "I'm sorry for your loss. As a single father, you can always adopt."

He stared at the fire in the fireplace. "Never."

She dropped her hand. "Why not?"

"He believes our parents adopted him out of a sense of duty to society, which couldn't be more wrong. Although they led fulfilling lives, they wanted to share their home with children." Jaclyn arched a carrot-red brow in Luciano's direction. "He still grieves the loss of his birth parents."

"Enough, Jaclyn. I wasn't brought to America until I was four years old. I have good memories of my childhood home in Italy before being left in that neglectful orphanage." The smooth, impassive features were back in place. He focused his gaze on Anastasia. "So why *are* you meeting with Sam tomorrow?"

Anastasia flinched and briefly closed her eyes. She didn't care about Justin anymore, so that certainly wasn't the reason. Their final conversation before their divorce had sparked a wound that wouldn't heal. She replayed his harsh and condescending words in her mind.

She'd lain in a hospital bed after the excisional surgery. *"But why do you want Eliza and not me?"* she'd asked. *"I'm your wife. We adopted a beautiful child together."*

She cringed. She'd been pathetic. Blame her sorrow on the resultant weakness after her surgery, the feeling of defeat. Never again, she vowed to herself. She'd rely only on herself.

"It's not that I don't love you," Justin had explained. *"It's just that I love Eliza more."*

Then he'd walked out of the hospital room. Anastasia's mind had been numb for days.

She took a long breath and pushed the devastating exchange aside. Prompted by the awful memory, the idea that had consumed her when he'd married Eliza came tumbling out. "I want to be awarded sole custody of Soo-Min."

Luciano tapped his fingers on his thigh. "Your daughter's best interests will be better served if she's raised by two united parents."

Anastasia dug her nails into her palms. "After years of endless affairs, Justin married a woman who's immature and irresponsible." Her voice shook as she spoke. "At first I agreed to the court's decision regarding joint custody, but in hindsight, I know that neither Justin nor Eliza deserves parenting time with my sweet, impressionable daughter."

Luciano raised a cool, challenging brow. "Your unbiased opinion, I presume?"

She sank back into the couch. "My daughter's an adoptee. Who knows what type of life she experienced in her Korean foster home before arriving in America? Those first few months are crucial to a child's development. She deserves unconditional affection and constant protection. Justin and his latest love provide neither."

"I lived in an orphanage. I turned out okay," Luciano replied.

"You always said you felt like an underdog and didn't belong anywhere," Jaclyn piped in. Then, she slapped a hand to her forehead. "In all this excitement, I forgot to mention that Sam's office called earlier. His schedule changed and he's out of town until next week. He had to meet with some big-shot client in Las Vegas, a movie star." She fiddled with the sleeves of her sweatshirt, exposing matching butterfly tattoos on each wrist.

Luciano smirked. "Still sizing him up as an eligible bachelor?"

"So sometimes he's not that dependable," Jaclyn agreed. "Nonetheless, he's still rich. He might even be richer than you."

Anastasia put her face in her hands. "Meeting with Sam is one of the main reasons I came to Charleston."

"Why don't you set up counsel with Liz, instead?" Luciano asked. "She's probably available."

Jaclyn swung him a knowing look. "She's always available, especially for you."

"We're just friends," he countered.

"Does she specialize in child custody disputes?" Anastasia asked.

"Although she's practicing law part-time, she seems to be always seeking new clients." With that, Jaclyn stood. "I'll take the dog for a walk. When I return, I'll drive you to your aunt's house, then I'll stop at Liz's place and set up a consultation for you tomorrow. Sound like a plan?"

"You can drop me at my office in town," Luciano said. "One of my computer files might still have my project notes. Providing I can get the generator to work, I'll be able to power it on. I have a small apartment in my building, so I'll stay there for the night."

Jaclyn pulled on a bright-yellow raincoat, matching rain boots, and then leashed the dog. She flicked on a light switch in the hall and shook her head. "Why do I flick on light switches when I know there's no power?" Muttering to herself, she grabbed a flashlight. "The flights in and out of Charleston airport were canceled. Your meeting will definitely be delayed."

Anastasia's stomach rumbled. "Is there anything in the fridge?"

Jaclyn shrugged, gave an exaggerated leap over the toilet in the foyer, then stepped out the door.

Luciano took the bag of ice off Anastasia's ankle. "I'll go check. Knowing my sister, any food will be either extremely healthy or extremely unhealthy."

CHAPTER SEVEN

A few minutes later, Luciano returned to the living room. "I found dry celery stalks and bottled water in the fridge, so unfortunately we caught the healthy week. I threw the celery in the bin."

Anastasia smiled and levered herself up to accept the water. "Water is good, thanks." She drank greedily, then placed the bottle on the coffee table. "Although a Sea Salt caramel would've been wonderful."

He loaded several small pieces of wood into the fireplace to keep the fire burning and settled beside her. She didn't acknowledge him, just stared at the flicks of curling flame. The firelight complemented her flawless complexion, the warm glow illuminating her exquisite features. He gazed at her silky, honey-brown hair fastened at the crown with one of Jaclyn's hair clips. The style accented her finely sculpted cheekbones.

"Are you missing your daughter?" he asked.

"Yes, very much. I should've never left Vermont."

His first impulse was to pull back in case she became too weepy.

"You came here to consult with Sam," he said. "You'll want to be armed with his extensive knowledge before opening a custody dispute."

"Yes, but there were other reasons why I came to Charleston, selfish ones. Do you want to know something?" She turned. Her magnificent eyes sparkled with tears. "I was afraid I would've bumped into Eliza bringing Soo-Min to the local art center or movie theater. Stowe's a small town," she whispered. "And I wouldn't have been able to bear the pain of seeing them together."

His arm slid around her, the instinct to comfort her coming naturally to him. He offered quiet encouragement and she accepted, pouring her tears into his chest. When her crying subsided, he tipped her chin up and smoothed the wetness from the corners of her eyes "Can I ask you something?"

She sniffed and nodded.

"Why did you pursue international adoption if your marriage was so troubled?"

Her gaze shadowed with hurt, and for a moment he chided himself. She was worn out and all the more sensitive to criticism. She needed rest and comfort, not condemnation.

She drew an unsteady breath and squarely met his gaze. "Because I desperately wanted a child and had exhausted all the other options. Justin and I were infertile as a couple. Thirty years old was a number that was nearing, and my biological clock ticked a little too loudly. I felt like a failure because I wasn't able to get pregnant."

"You're not a failure, and there's nothing shameful about infertility."

She looked away. "And if I'm completely honest with myself, some small part of me hoped that a child might save my marriage."

Luciano took her cold hands in his. "That admittance takes a great deal of courage."

"Thanks." She regarded him with a teary smile. "And then Soo-Min arrived at the New York airport, and you know what? Everything changed. All the heartache, the fighting with Justin, everything. I remember that day so well. She was ten months old and was escorted by an elderly Korean man, along with three other babies. She was adorable, dressed in a bright-pink Korean Hanbok, which is a traditional Korean dress. Immediately, I fell in love with her."

His brows drew together. "I love your story, I really do. But I don't agree with adopting internationally."

Her eyes narrowed. "You, of all people. Why, you're an international adoptee yourself!"

"I've researched and read countless studies. International adoptions aren't fair to the child because it displaces that child from a true home environment and culture."

"And there are many other articles proving otherwise," she countered. "Your adoptive parents were wonderful and caring. I was at your house many times hanging out with Jaclyn. Your childhood was filled with affection and couldn't have been more perfect."

He pressed a kiss on her forehead, hoping to take the sting from his words. She'd confided in him. The shared trust and understanding they'd begun to build again after all these years apart could easily crumble. "You're absolutely right. I loved my adoptive parents very much and miss them more each day."

"Your opinions are contrary to what I believe." Her gaze shimmered with understanding. "Although I know you miss your adoptive parents."

"They tried, you know? However, I've never recovered from the ache in my gut that my birth family abandoned me," he admitted, underlining his words. "The memory of living in a tiny apartment in Italy haunts me every day. I can still smell the meatballs in a tomato and garlic sauce simmering on the stove." He drew in a deep breath. "All my life I've been searching for something, although I don't know what I was looking for. Perhaps the answer lies in Italy, my birthplace."

He'd said too much, divulging a sadness he'd never shared. He focused on a hole in the ceiling.

"Everyone's curious about his or her heritage. Someday, you'll find information about your birth family and you're bound to be pleased, for their kind hearts will surely match yours."

He cleared his throat. "I've searched exhaustively and hired thirty investigators, but they haven't found any information. The adoption agency in Italy said that the records had been sealed."

"Keep trying."

He intended to, using all his money and resources. When he found his birth family, he'd buy them all a home and throw a celebration. In fact, he'd buy the entire Italian town.

"Meanwhile, I'll be the perfect mother for my daughter in the perfect little town."

He chuckled. "I lived in that snowy little town for many years, and it isn't my idea of perfect."

She granted him a sweet, genuine smile and rested her head against his chest. "When you and I were younger, we talked like this all the time, remember? I'd complain endlessly about my lonely home life, and you'd sit and listen and encourage me."

He stroked an errant fringe of side swept bangs

away from her face. He noticed the small scar and didn't comment. "I admired your perseverance. You were fearless."

After a moment, she murmured, "I wasn't fearless. I wanted a happy family."

He gathered her in his arms. "Close your eyes."

She chuckled and complied.

He whispered close to her ear. "I enjoyed every one of our conversations, although I never would've admitted it back then."

She opened her eyes. "And now?"

"Nothing's changed," he recognized. She was still the provocative, exhilarating woman he'd admired sixteen years ago.

It was as if they'd resumed where they'd left off, conversing on his back porch after his boxing matches, her long hair pulled up in a damp ponytail, her cheeks flushed from the exertion of a hard swim practice.

She slanted an audacious smile at him. "Where were you sixteen years ago when I needed you?"

"I'm here for you now, *Mia Cara*. Never forget that."

Without his urging, she tipped her face up to his. He gathered her close and pressed his lips against her forehead, her hair. Ever so gently, his thumbs stroked the freckles on her cheeks.

Her lips parted and she sighed. Her arms glided around his neck and his mouth moved to capture hers. He caught her arms and pulled her onto his lap. "You'll be more comfortable." He offered a charming, teasing smile. Looping his arms around her, he drew her near and kissed her deeply. His blood hammered as she melted her provocative body against his.

The front door burst open.

"I'm home!" Jaclyn stopped short in the entryway and unleashed Lady. The dog, all sixty pounds of her, bounded through the foyer to jump on the couch.

Luciano expelled a long breath. Anastasia attempted to lurch to a sitting position, but he kept her on his lap.

Jaclyn strolled into the living room. "I doubt there's any hot water, although I'm showering anyway before I drive Anastasia to her aunt and uncle's house." She grinned. "Unless, of course, my big brother needs that cold shower first."

CHAPTER EIGHT

Gripping a flashlight and overnight bag packed with a set of Jaclyn's clothes and toiletries, Anastasia stood at the doorway to her aunt and uncle's townhouse and knocked on the door. Although the rain had lessened, evidence of the storm shone from the burning candles flickering through the windows. Apparently, most of Charleston was still without power.

A short, stubby woman with salt-and-pepper hair flung open the door and ushered Anastasia inside the tiny foyer. Her plump face wreathed into a smile. "Thank goodness you're safe. I was so worried, I was driving your uncle crazy."

"I had no way to reach you. I know my visit tonight is unexpected but—"

"Why didn't you call when you arrived in Charleston?"

"Sorry, the afternoon went by so fast and then my cell phone lost power. In fact, it was swept away by the hurricane." Anastasia placed a kiss on her aunt's cheek and hugged her. "Do you have a working landline? I need to call my ex's house."

"The phone's in the kitchen," Uncle Filipp called from the living room. "Grab some pasta salad and tea while you're in there."

"Thanks." Anastasia pointed to the smart car idling in the driveway. "Jaclyn dropped me off. Can I stay the night?"

"Of course. We have a spare bedroom. There's so much to catch up on," her aunt said.

Anastasia set her bag in the foyer, steeling herself for her aunt's interrogations sure to follow. She lingered at the doorway and waved to Jaclyn and Luciano as they backed out of the driveway. "See you tomorrow!"

Luciano rolled down the car window. "May I take you to lunch at one of my favorite restaurants in Charleston?" he asked in a deep, polite voice that brooked no dispute. She noted the guarded hope in his gaze along with his lazy smile, and her heart gave an unexpected lurch.

She returned his smile. "Yes, I'll look forward to it." She paused by the entry door as the car sped away, then closed the door and crossed the foyer into the living room.

"I swear if another storm comes through, I'll never recover from the fright. I told your uncle we should've moved to Florida," Aunt Irina was saying. "I was torn between screaming my head off or fainting dead away every time the wind roared through here."

"Believe me, when I saw a dome of ocean waves, I felt the same way," Anastasia replied.

Uncle Filipp came to his feet and peered at Anastasia above his reading glasses. "You look like you walked through a hurricane."

"I did, actually. And ran, and swam and screamed bloody terror." She pecked a kiss on her uncle's forehead and headed for the kitchen to call Soo-Min. Then, because she'd memorized the number, she'd call her bank to cancel her credit cards. She'd brave the long lines at the DMV for a new license when she returned to Stowe.

After five rings, Eliza answered groggily. "Your number came up on the caller ID. Why are you calling so late?"

"Haven't you heard? A hurricane came through Charleston."

A hesitation. "I didn't see anything on the news," Eliza said.

"Can I speak with my daughter?" Anastasia asked.

"It's midnight and I put her to bed hours ago. I must've read that book about the furry barnyard animals three times before she finally went to sleep. I'm certainly not waking her up."

"Eliza, please ..." Anastasia swallowed. "It's been a rough day. I want to hear my daughter's voice."

"Sorry," Eliza responded in a sharp tone. "Disrupting her from a deep sleep won't accomplish anything except make you feel better. Call back in the morning."

The phone clicked. Anastasia stared at the receiver and shook her head.

She stepped into the living room while balancing a tray containing a plate of pasta salad, a fork and two china cups brimming with hot tea. She offered one cup to her aunt, then sank into a shiny turquoise rocking chair. Anastasia placed her teacup and pasta on the coffee table.

Aunt Irina, comfortably ensconced on a worn plaid sofa, peered at Anastasia over the rim of her steaming cup. "By the look on your face, dear, I'm assuming your call to Justin didn't go well."

"I wanted to talk to my daughter. However, Eliza wouldn't allow it." Anastasia's vision blurred and she wiped hastily at her eyes. "I suppose it's my fault because I didn't realize how late it was."

Uncle Filipp shot her aunt an exasperated look. "Let your skinny niece eat. She looks terrible."

Anastasia bit back a grin and reached for the

pasta. "Thanks for all the compliments, Uncle Filipp."

"Who was that man in the car?" her aunt asked. "He looked like Jaclyn's brother."

"Yes, that man was Luciano."

"I remember him. Wasn't he captain of the football team?"

"He was captain of the boxing club," Anastasia corrected. "Jaclyn lives with him while her home is being renovated. Except now, she has a home and he doesn't." Anastasia tightened her grip on her fork as the emotional stress of the day's events hurtled through her mind.

"Isn't their last name 'Donati'?" her uncle asked. "There's an impressive office complex downtown with that name emblazoned across the front. Some software company."

Anastasia nodded and took a bite of pasta. "That's probably Luciano's office. Jaclyn said he's on his way to becoming a billionaire."

Her heart swelled with pride as she spoke because he'd earned his success on his own. Of everyone she'd ever known, Luciano was the one person who could accomplish such a remarkable feat. He was sharp and witty, brilliant yet infuriating.

She sighed and shrugged that last thought aside. She believed in him, admired him. He always made her laugh, despite the circumstances. And he'd be the first to poke fun at himself.

"I lived in an orphanage, not a beach resort," he'd wryly observed.

Her cheeks heated, remembering his lips moving tenderly over hers.

"I always liked him." Aunt Irina proffered her broadest grin. "Whenever he came home from college, he'd attend your swim meets."

Anastasia shook her head. "You must be mixing him up with someone else. He never attended my meets."

Her aunt downed a generous gulp of tea, then set down her cup and pushed up the sleeves of her flowing housecoat. "He stood in the sidelines near the edge of the bleachers. Sometimes we talked about the back-breaking factory work and deafening conditions that he and your mother endured, although Luciano was determined to help his parents pay for his college. I'm surprised he never mentioned our conversations to you."

Anastasia smiled kindly at her elderly aunt and didn't argue with her reflections. She was obviously mistaken.

Her aunt bestowed an exaggerated wink. "What brings you to Charleston besides that good-looking billionaire? When you called me last week from Vermont, you said you'd explain when you got here."

Quickly, Anastasia recounted the circumstances of why she planned to petition the court for full custody of Soo-Min, explaining Jaclyn's recommenda-tion to meet with Sam for a free consultation.

"Free or not, there's no reason to consult with a lawyer from another state, plus you want the home town advantage." Uncle Filipp held his fingers loosely behind his back. "Your parenting plan with Justin was approved by the court for joint custody."

Anastasia nodded. "I'm planning to request a modification. Besides—"

He checked her explanation in mid-sentence. "Your relationship with Justin is good and he pays child support?"

"Yes. However, his new wife is too young and im-mature to parent properly."

Aunt Irina sank her sturdy body farther down into the couch. Two spots of vibrant-pink appeared on her well-rounded cheeks. "We've all witnessed Justin's bad temper on several family occasions. Nevertheless, he's obviously a good father who's devoted to Soo-Min. Still, who can predict how a man will retaliate if he fears losing the privilege of seeing his child?"

Uncle Filipp lifted a bushy brow at his wife's out-burst, then frowned at Anastasia. "You're no fool. However, what if you lose the custody hearing? You smoothly navigated the international adoption process, but Soo-Min may be caught in an angry dis-pute with your ex which may drag on for years."

"And what about your cancer, dear?" Aunt Irina's

mouth took a grim twist. "Your mother would've been so concerned about your receiving the best possible treatment if she were still alive."

Anastasia jabbed at her pasta with a fork. "I'm cancer-free and doubt she would've noticed any signs of melanoma."

"She was a single mother struggling to make ends meet and working long hours. Your swim meets were very costly," her aunt countered. "She paid for all the expenses on her own."

Anastasia set her plate on the table and went for her cup of tea. "Aunt Irina, I appreciated that you attended my meets, but my mother wasn't there. I'd look up before I dove into the water for my freestyle swim event and never saw her. I was her only child and she never sat in the stands cheering for me. Family should've been more important than working in that awful factory or staying out late with her boyfriend. I sat alone in an empty house my entire childhood. Besides—"

Her aunt cut off Anastasia's next sentence with a sweep of her arms. "She tried her best and worked hard."

"Perhaps." Anastasia sat straighter. "Although you can be sure that my daughter's childhood will be different." She set her teacup clattering on the saucer and rubbed the back of her neck. "I intend to be an outstanding mother and provide a stable, nurturing home. I've read all the latest parenting books and scoured the websites. I'm prepared."

"Like your mother, you're a single parent," Uncle Filipp said in a sharp tone. "Without any support, you'll face financial challenges. And who'll help with the day-to-day responsibilities?"

Anastasia summoned a brave smile. "I plan to return to teaching. The elementary school where I worked several years ago offers an excellent after school day care. Soo-Min will enter Kindergarten in the fall, and she can attend school there. They assured me I could return whenever I wished."

"You're assuming there's a job opening waiting for you and not taking into account that there may not be any vacancies. But let's hope you're right, because you'll need money. The cost of all those court hearings and missed work days will cost thousands of dollars," Uncle Filipp said.

Anastasia opened her mouth to refute him, although Aunt Irina interrupted with a glare aimed at Uncle Filipp. "Our niece is obviously exhausted, and she's endured more than enough anxiety for one day." Aunt Irina stood, lifted her dainty teacup for another gulp that wasn't there, and scowled into the empty cup.

. . .

*I*n the spare bedroom, Anastasia slid off the snug tunic and sweat pants borrowed from Jaclyn, took a quick shower and donned a night shirt. She'd placed one lit candle on the dresser, then covered a yawn with her hand, although she felt too wound up for sleep.

Absently, she scratched the mole near her wrist, then sat on the bed to inspect it. The mole was scaly and felt tender. Perhaps she'd scraped it when she'd slipped and fallen on Luciano's concrete deck, although she didn't remember hurting her wrist, only her ankle. Still, the day had brought fright and turmoil, so unexpected injuries were expected.

She stretched out her legs. The lilac-flowered comforter had been turned down, and the cozy bed beckoned. Sleep would restore her spirits and sweep away her fatigue. She slipped between the covers and closed her eyes, seeking comforting dreams.

Hours later, she lay awake on her stomach and listened to the sound of rain drumming against the windows.

She'd been convinced she was doing the right thing in pursuing a custody dispute, for a proper home situation was in Soo-Min's best interests, wasn't it? She mulled over the conversation with her aunt and uncle and couldn't fault their opinions because they offered logical advice. Could she, in fact, juggle the challenges of parenting while working full-time, without a husband or family support network to share the workload?

She rolled to her back. She'd planned it all—the white picket fence, two adorable children, a loving husband. However, life hadn't happened the way she'd planned. That perfect family she'd always wanted was an elusive dream.

She placed her hands behind her head and stared at the ceiling. What did a perfect family even look like, anyway? She bit her lip and sighed.

With a strong frown and stronger opinions, Luciano had voiced disapproval regarding adoption, although Anastasia reasoned that his opinions were spurred more from his own inner conflicts. His adoptive parents had been kind, encouraging and clearly loved their children. For a man so brilliant, didn't he realize that his experience as an adoptee contradicted his research?

She didn't fault his resolve to travel to Italy. In fact, she'd encouraged him to research his heritage. He'd once told her that he dreamed of someday having a loving wife and several children. Optimistically, his search would reunite him with many Italian aunts and uncles and boisterous cousins.

During the summer as a young man, he'd spent endless hours tutoring neighborhood children in math, his obvious forte. If a child needed extra help, Luciano would give up time at his beloved boxing gym. There was no doubt that he'd be a wonderful father.

And then there was Luciano, the man. Despite the terrifying day they'd shared, she'd felt safe with him. His calmness disarmed her, even when she was so frightened she could hardly string two thoughts together. And throughout their ordeal, she'd felt him watching her, protectively. She'd trust him with her life. Always had.

Sixteen years ago, he'd never given her reason to believe he was interested in her romantically. Nevertheless, there was no mistaking his expression tonight before he'd kissed her. He cared for her, and not just as an old friend anymore. And if she examined her feelings, she knew she'd always cared for him. The handsome college sophomore she'd had a mad crush on had become more sophisticated, more exasperating, and even more vital.

"Mia Cara," he'd whispered, his gaze dark with concern. He'd bent to check her ankle and rubbed the soreness away.

They'd enjoyed a comfortable friendship in their youth, and that friendship had deepened. The guarded hope in his expression when he'd invited her to lunch was unmistakable. She knew he was eager to see her again. And she was just as eager to see him.

CHAPTER NINE

*L*uciano glanced at the enormous oak wall clock chiming noon in the lobby of the Fullman law offices. He shifted, unbuttoned his navy sports jacket and shoved his hands into the pockets of his gray flannel pants. For the third time in fifteen minutes, he'd peered out the large front window, waiting for Jaclyn to drive up in her smart car with Anastasia. He'd given his sister hundreds of dollars, insisting that she and Anastasia shop at several boutiques on King Street for new wardrobes. Anastasia had lost literally the clothes on her back, her purse, wallet, and personal belongings since arriving in Charleston. She hadn't seemed concerned about her material possessions, valuing only her daughter's baby pictures.

He smiled, outrageously pleased with the principled, honorable woman she'd become. Dauntingly fearless during the hurricane, she'd trusted his instructions to open the door and let in more water even though the Hummer was clearly sinking. She'd also bravely rescued his dog as the storm roared and a dome of water rushed toward them. Afterwards, she'd slogged through blocks of floodwater without a word of complaint, despite her sprained ankle and the weariness displayed on her pale features.

He yanked off his sports jacket, placed it on an expensive antique chair and strolled closer to the window. His frustration regarding the postponed board meeting with his investors was compounded by canceled plane flights and rescheduling conflicts. Fortunately, he'd been able to retrieve most of the project information from his office computer.

Earlier in the morning, he'd filed insurance claims for his home, possessions and Hummer. His lease on a new BMW was promised by late afternoon. He'd need to drive to the island with the insurance agent to assess the devastation to his home and property.

He rubbed his jaw. Sometimes he considered leaving all the meetings and schedules and tension behind and living a simpler lifestyle. Were his possessions and success truly bringing joy? Would peace, a cheery fireplace and an exhilarating woman by his side take away the wounds of being relinquished and abandoned as a child?

He kept his gaze fixed on the window. Where were they? He was eager to see Anastasia and show her Charleston. After her consultation with Liz, he'd take her to lunch at one of his favorite restaurants, perhaps taking a horse-drawn carriage ride afterward. Although the skies still growled with gray skies, the afternoon with Anastasia would be perfect.

Despite their ordeal yesterday, he couldn't stop gazing at her. Her beauty had matured to an unassuming grace, her face reflected the years in between with both resolve and heartache. It was no secret that her daughter was her primary concern and she'd soon be leaving Charleston behind.

He crossed his arms. Just why her leaving bothered him was something he couldn't explain. He told himself it was because they were old friends, recently reunited, and there was so much more to talk about because they never ran out of words when they were together.

But there was more, he knew there was more. Her teasing smile warmed his soul. Her light touch ignited his desire. She was unpretentious and sincere, unaffected by her good looks, gazing tenderly into his eyes when he'd kissed her. She loved life and laughter and his teasing jokes.

He stared out the window and ran a hand over his bristled jaw. Several palm trees swayed fitfully, a harsh reminder of the after-effects of a hurricane.

Anastasia's musical laughter from the day before paraded through his mind. *"You really get a charge out of your own humor."* His mind riveted to the way she'd looked as she lay on the chaise lounge on his balcony, the blue knit sundress clinging to her curves, her face flushed from sleep. The thought of never seeing her again left a pang of loneliness he couldn't shake. After sixteen years, how could he lose her a second time?

Liz walked into the lobby from another office and glanced at the bright overhead lights. "Well, at least the power was restored early this morning. Without it, I wouldn't have been able to see any clients today. I look a fright when I can't use a curling iron on my hair."

He bestowed an indulgent smile in her direction, taking in her lush blonde curls and the two carat diamond earrings gleaming from each ear.

"You realize I'm offering this free consultation as a favor to you and Jaclyn," Liz added.

Luciano grinned unapologetically. "And because your brother canceled. Anastasia flew in from Vermont specifically to speak with him."

"You're placing quite a priority on this woman. Who is she again?" Liz asked.

"An old friend," was all he said while he continued to peer out the lobby window. With a smile, he noted the metallic-red smart car pulling up to the curb.

When Anastasia entered the lobby, laughing and chatting with Jaclyn, his heart stopped in his throat. She looked exquisite. He strode to her and took her hands in his. They were so close that his shirt brushed against her sweater. "You look like a Greek goddess," he said.

"Thank you, although it's embarrassing to compete with a handsome Greek god." She grinned. "Have you been waiting long for me?" She glanced around. Apparently suddenly aware of Jaclyn and Liz staring at them, Anastasia withdrew her hands and stepped back. She wore a breezy maxi sundress in smoky blue-gray to match her exquisite eyes, her slim waist accentuated by a leopard belt. A loosely knit cream sweater covered her trim arms, and black suede ankle-tie shoes and a patent-leather purse completed the outfit. As usual, she wore no jewelry.

Once, she'd explained that her high school swim coach forbade the swimmers to wear jewelry, even a hair band. Apparently, Anastasia had grown accustomed to the absence of jewelry. He wondered if she'd worn a wedding ring when she was married.

A knowing smile touched Jaclyn's lips as she extended a hand toward Anastasia, who blushed attractively. "Quite a transformation from the woman you saw last night, big brother. I've officially introduced Anastasia to designer fashion." Jaclyn twirled, calling attention to her poppy-colored floral sundress and white sneakers. "We happily spent all your money."

Luciano grinned at Anastasia. "My money was well spent."

"I'm not used to wearing such expensive clothes. Suppose I spill something on them?"

"Then my brother will buy you another outfit," Jaclyn provided.

Liz focused an icy look at Jaclyn. "Well, now that we've enjoyed your fashion commentary, we can get started." She stepped forward, extended a hand toward Anastasia, and said flatly, "I'm Liz Fullman."

Anastasia smiled and accepted the woman's handshake, apparently impervious to Liz's razor-edged gaze. "I'm Anastasia Markow."

She'd used her maiden name, he smiled inwardly. She had so much spirit, staying true to her convictions to create a better, independent life for herself and her daughter.

He picked up his sports jacket, brushing a kiss on Anastasia's forehead. "I'll walk to my office and return within the hour. My secretary is attempting to reschedule the board meeting for some time later this week." He gave a brief wave and headed out the door.

"And I'm off to my travel agency to book a cruise, then on to my canoeing lesson with my hunky new teacher. I thought I knew everything about canoeing, but he's teaching me new skills." Jaclyn turned to Anastasia and Liz. "Enjoy your expensive lunch at The Turning Rhinestone!"

Liz sighed. "My favorite restaurant, although I'm taking a train to Vegas tonight to assist Sam in a high profile case. He knows I can't resist movie stars. He's not famous yet. However, he's had a one-line part in a couple of big movies."

"You weren't invited to lunch, Liz," Jaclyn corrected with a teasing smirk. "My brother wants Anastasia all to himself."

*A*nastasia followed Liz up the marble stairway to the second floor law offices. The woman was breathtaking, her lavish curves fitted in a pea-green silk dress, every inch the professional, accomplished woman.

Liz nodded to a secretary busily answering calls in one of the offices.

"Good afternoon, Ms. Fullman," the secretary said briskly, ignoring Anastasia.

At the end of the hall, Liz opened the door and flicked on the lights in a large conference room. One entire wall boasted a mural of the city of Charleston, and slightly curved chairs in chrome detailing surrounded a heavy oak table. Clearly, no expense had been spared to impress well-heeled clients.

Liz gestured toward a couple of wooden chairs and a desk in the corner. "Shut the door behind you," she instructed. She promenaded to the desk, seated herself and recovered a long sheet of paper from the bottom drawer. She requested Anastasia to sit across from her. Then she smiled and drawled, "I don't mind sharing him, you know."

Anastasia blinked. "I'm sorry, I don't understand."

"Of course you do. You're a beautiful divorcee with a small child appealing to him for help. Luciano would never refuse a sweet-talking-woman in distress."

Anastasia paused, settling her expensive patent leather purse on her lap, knowing Liz was waiting for an answer. "Luciano and I are old friends," she said cautiously

"You can enjoy him for the afternoon. I enjoyed his company last night."

Anastasia's head jerked up. Luciano had said he was spending the night at his office. He'd never mentioned that he'd planned on seeing Liz.

She pressed herself into the chair. With rising annoyance, she studied this elegantly coiffed blonde woman sitting across from her.

Seeing Luciano standing in the lobby, Anastasia's heart had skipped a beat. He'd never looked so handsome, his creamy-white polo shirt hugging his muscular, tanned arms, his long legs fitted in gray flannel pants, a shadow of a dark beard on his strong jaw. His bold gaze had roamed appreciatively over her body, then had captured her gaze with an approving smile. He'd tossed a navy sports coat over one shoulder, looking completely at ease in the richly-decorated lobby. He was every inch the successful millionaire and she was beginning to realize that he was completely out of her league, just as he'd always been. To make matters worse, Liz oozed self-assurance. And, she was more gorgeous than any other woman Anastasia had ever met.

"I've been filled in on your case," Liz said crisply, retrieving two additional pieces of stapled paper from her desk drawer. Apparently, she could switch to her professional persona without blinking. "You'll need to submit your modification custody request in writing to the Superior Court in Vermont. Expect a fee for filing, of course. And I assume it's been at least one year since your initial custody agreement?"

Anastasia bit her lip and nodded. "My divorce decree stated that I could revert back to my maiden name, which I did. I'd like to petition the court to change Soo-Min's last name to my maiden name, also. Currently, her last name is Parker, which is my ex's name."

Liz jotted notes on the paper. "Any domestic violence or child abuse?"

"No."

"Good. Otherwise there'd be an investigation, although be prepared for the court to call in a social service agency to evaluate your ex-husband's home situation. Your child's physical or emotional health isn't endangered when she's with him?"

"Justin's home situation is good, it's just that his new wife is so young and—"

Liz checked another box and glanced at her watch. "Has Justin disobeyed the custody agreement in any way?"

"No. He's very dependable." Anastasia braced her hands on the desk for support. "Do I have a case?"

Liz pushed that question aside with a wave of her hands. "Maybe. The court has the authority to decide, and the case will be determined by the best interests of the child."

Anastasia flinched, then straightened her shoulders and met Liz's indifferent gaze directly. "Of course, I want what's best for her. I'm her mother."

Luciano opened the door of Liz's office and strode in without knocking. Apparently, he was very comfortable in her office. He propped a shoulder against the wall and crossed his arms. "Making headway?"

"We're finished. Perfect timing, as always." Liz gave a stunning white smile accompanied by a throaty laugh as she shoved the papers aside. She handed Anastasia her business card and stood abruptly in an obvious attempt to dismiss Anastasia.

"Can you assist Anastasia with her case?" he asked.

"You wanted me to offer her my free expertise and I did, although all the courts respond differently. When are you filing, Anastasia?" Liz asked.

"I'd like to file as soon as I return to Vermont." Anastasia pushed back her chair, dangled the gold chain of her purse over her shoulder and stood. "Although I understand the need to fill out the form correctly and would prefer a lawyer present."

Luciano ran a hand through his hair. "Is it possible for you to fly to Vermont, Liz?"

Liz hurled an unapologetic excuse. "I'm sorry, I can't. The Clerk in Vermont will record the file and set a date for the first hearing. Perhaps at that time I can clear my schedule."

"Would you consider going to Vermont earlier if I came, too?" Luciano gave Anastasia a conspiratorial wink.

Liz's face brightened. "Perhaps you and I can ski while we're there."

"Perhaps." He strode to Anastasia and offered his hand. "Shall we go to lunch?"

Anastasia took his hand. "I'll ... I'll call you?" she asked Liz over her shoulder as she and Luciano walked out of the office.

Liz clasped her hands together in hopeful, mock anticipation. "You do that."

With a nod to the brisk secretary, Luciano and Anastasia crossed the hallway, down the lobby stairs and out the front door. The air smelled fresh and clean, the sky slowly clearing. They strolled past sleeping formal gardens and lush green manicured lawns, as well as stately homes graced with pillars.

Despite what Liz had insinuated regarding her night with Luciano, Anastasia dismissed the conversation. He wanted to have lunch with her, not Liz. His warm hand was clasped firmly around hers, not Liz's. And he'd help ensure that the court petition would be filed correctly in Vermont, the first step before the initial court appearance.

"As long as your ankle isn't bothering you, we'll walk a couple of more blocks to one of my favorite restaurants located in the peninsula. I reserved a small private dining room for us." He grinned boyishly. "Do you like steak and salad along with Italian food?"

"I like all kinds of food and especially salad. Which reminds me, I know a great joke. Want to hear it?"

He grinned. "Absolutely."

"What did the bacon say to the tomato?"

She was rewarded by his deep chuckle. "That's an easy one. Lettuce get together."

A few minutes later they arrived at The Turning Rhinestone, a Charleston institution. Arched windows and the warm scent of wood-burning fireplaces greeted them.

"These heart-pine floors are one hundred years old," Luciano said as they were led to an exclusive private room in the back of the restaurant. He seemed unaware of the stir he was causing while several uniformed waiters whispered approvingly.

After they were seated and given menus, Luciano grinned at her with a gleam in his eye. "Is it too soon for hurricane jokes, or should we wait for everything to blow over?"

"Only if it's been downgraded to a tropical depression," she laughed.

His expression softened. "Are you recovered from yesterday's ordeal, *Mia Cara*?"

Mia Cara. Her breath came out ragged as she nodded.

"Good. Because I want to kiss you."

She looked around the fancy surroundings and shook her head. "Not here."

"I've never been one to listen to advice." He leaned over the table and cupped her chin, his lips moving firmly against hers.

A white-shirted waiter approached carrying a silver platter with menus and two fluted glasses, one filled with champagne, the other with ice water. He politely cleared his throat and set the glasses on the table.

Feeling her face flush, Anastasia smoothed her dress while attempting a gracious inclination of her head.

"The reservation stated this is a celebration luncheon, Mr. Donati?" the waiter asked.

"Yes." Luciano smiled and sat. "Ms. Markow and I survived yesterday's hurricane intact. We've been apart for sixteen years, so this lunch is a celebration of our reunion."

"Very good, sir." The waiter handed them menus.

Once the a la carte entrees were explained and orders placed, Luciano asked, "How is your daughter faring without you?"

Anastasia perched her chin on her hands. "I called her this morning from my aunt's house while Jaclyn took your dog for a walk. Soo-Min said she missed me, although she sounded happy. I'm anxious to return home and see her, then begin custody proceedings."

He reached for her hand and gave an encouraging squeeze. "Liz will offer legal expertise, and I'll come along for moral support." He lifted his glass and prompted her to do the same.

"A toast to spirited friendships and forever friends." A quiet smile kindled in his espresso-colored gaze as they clinked glasses. "May I have the good fortune to win a special woman's loyal heart, and the worthiness to deserve her love."

CHAPTER TEN

*L*unch was an extravagant affair which began
with jumbo shrimp cocktail appetizers and
a chopped green salad, followed by crispy
crab cakes seared to perfection, and creamy whipped
potatoes.

Luciano's perfectly cooked steak arrived sizzling
at the table. Carrots in a soy glaze and thick cut fries
accompanied his meal. Hardly Italian cuisine, nonetheless, the meal was exquisitely satisfying and delicious.

A rich, creamy rice dish was offered for dessert,
which they shared.

Full to bursting, Anastasia eagerly accepted Luciano's offer to walk and show her the streets of
Charleston. They strolled aimlessly hand in hand
while he pointed out important monuments and dis-

tinguished museums, his delight infectious. He glanced at his watch as they walked toward the historic district. "Would you like to take a carriage ride before dark?"

She stopped to admire an iron gate adorned with a flower box filled with purple pansies and couldn't help her smile, thinking of Jaclyn's romance comment regarding good-looking men in horse-drawn carriages. She hesitated, prolonging the moment. "I'd love a carriage ride with you."

They strode to the end of a cobbled street where horses with carriages were lined. Luciano assisted her into the leather seat of the carriage, then sat beside her. His arm possessively went around her shoulders, and she turned into his warm body and reassuring strength.

"I'm looking forward to visiting you in Vermont," he said. "I haven't been back there since I graduated from college."

"Will you arrive in time for your Valentine's Day birthday?" she asked.

He sat back and grinned. "How did you know about my birthday?"

"Jaclyn told me."

He shook his head. "I should've known."

"Soo-Min's a wonderful little helper in the kitchen and loves to lick the icing off the mixing spoon," Anastasia said. "I took a cake decorating course a few years ago, so be prepared for a fancy cake." Inwardly, she smiled. Years ago, she'd purchased a heart-shaped baking tin and never used it. She visualized a three-tiered cake adorned with chocolate curls and butter cream frosting.

"We bake a sour cream chocolate cake to die for," she added.

"I like vanilla."

She burst out laughing. "Do you like strawberry jam? I can spread it between the layers."

"Chocolate or vanilla layers?"

"I'm a versatile baker and can make an equally delicious vanilla layer cake."

"Perfect." He leaned over and his mouth slowly descended on hers. "Remember, I like anything sweet."

The carriage jolted forward, sweeping through a main iron gate, and the good-natured driver pointed out rows of rainbow-colored houses. Glimmering lights began to shine from the homes, signaling the approach of dusk. The flame from the coach lamps flickered rhythmically with each clip-clop of the horses' hooves.

"Before I forget, we should exchange cell phone numbers." Luciano dropped his arm and pulled out his cell phone. "I'll give you my office number, also."

She plugged his numbers into the new cell phone she'd purchased that morning. He plugged in hers.

Her wrist itched. Without thinking, she absently scratched through her sweater, surprised to feel a wetness. She pushed up her sleeves and gasped. The mole on her wrist was scaly and oozing blood.

Luciano's gaze collided with hers. "When did that happen?" His dark brows drew together as he lifted her wrist and examined the mole.

She yanked free from his grasp. "I've had the mole for years and noticed it was swollen shortly after arriving at your house yesterday. I'm sure it's nothing, although I'll call Dr. Leskin when I get back home. He's my family doctor."

Luciano withdrew a handkerchief from his sports jacket and pressed it against her wrist. "You're going home immediately to have this mole checked by a specialist." He rapped for the driver to stop the carriage. "We're taking a taxi back to your aunt and uncle's house. Then I'm putting you on the first and fastest train out of Charleston."

She looked down and pressed her hands to her temples. No. Not again. The surgical excision, the scarring, the talk of safety margins and healthy-looking skin tissue also removed. She couldn't face the terrifying prospect alone.

"Are you able to come with me?" Her voice choked, she was shaking. She sounded desperate. Pathetic. Again. She closed her eyes. *Rely on yourself.*

When she opened her eyes, Luciano was gazing intently at her and shaking his head. "I can't. I want to .... but I can't. My secretary was able to move the board meeting to tomorrow. The investors rescheduled other appointments to accommodate me and I can't cancel."

No one had ever supported her when she was sick. Slowly, she shook her head and a heaviness filled her body. "I understand."

"I'll fly to Vermont as soon as my investors and I come to an agreement," Luciano was saying. He was offering false hope and a weak smile. He'd explained the reasons why he was uncomfortable around hospitals and doctors. He didn't like the feeling of being powerless, and the gut-wrenching memories.

So, in the end, despite his good intentions, his good reasons, his good excuses, he wouldn't come.

She swallowed hard. "I'll miss you."

CHAPTER ELEVEN

*W*ith a thin cover draped around her naked body, Anastasia sat shivering in the office examining room, waiting for Dr. Bon, the dermatologist, to scrape the top layer of the mole on her wrist after the anesthetic took hold. At Luciano's insistence, her family doctor, Dr. Leskin, had referred her to the specialist.

"As you know from your previous history, this is a minor biopsy which my office will send to the lab," Dr. Bon explained. "We should get results back in a week. If it's suspicious, we'll schedule an appointment to remove the rest of the mole."

She nodded and thanked him as he left room. Dr. Bon had inspected every inch of her body. Fortunately, he'd found no other suspicious moles.

She inched off the examining table and hurriedly

dressed, anxious to pick up her daughter. The previous day, she'd gotten off the train in Vermont and
arrived on Justin's doorstep soon afterward. He'd
been surprised to see her several days earlier than
planned, but Eliza had seemed relieved that her
week entertaining a four-year-old child had ended.

Soo-Min had greeted Anastasia's return with a
scream of delight. She'd broken into an enormous
smile, then bombarded Anastasia with questions
about Charleston.

Anastasia retrieved her phone from her purse.
There were no calls from Justin, who'd agreed to
watch Soo-Min for the appointment, although there
were three text messages from Luciano:

'I'm thinking about you. Are you at your appointment? Text me.'

'These pompous board members insist on dragging these endless meetings one more day. Text me.'

And finally, 'Where are you? Text me.'

A few minutes later, she ducked into her car and
texted him back: 'Dr. Bon scraped the mole and is
sending it to the lab. He'll call when the results
come back in a week.'

Immediately, Luciano responded: 'I've booked
the first flight out of Charleston to Vermont the day
after tomorrow and arrive at ten o'clock in the
morning. Can you pick me up at the Burlington
airport?'

'Yes,' her fingers typed quickly. "Soo-Min will be

with me. She's still off from preschool because of winter break.'

She waited several minutes for his next reply and tapped her fingers on the steering wheel to pass the time. Finally, he texted: 'Looking forward to it.'

No words were added regarding when Liz was flying to Vermont to file the appeal.

Sighing, she eased her car out of the parking lot into traffic. A forty-five minute car ride from Burlington with Luciano and her chatty daughter should prove to be an adventure. She smiled at the thought.

"*H*i, Mr. Luciano, I'm Soo-Min. What's your favorite color? I like blue."

Luciano gazed at the adorable little girl sporting straight, shiny-black bangs and wild pigtails, hopping on one foot at the Burlington airport. She held up a sign pointing to thick letters scrawled in Crayola-blue, reading, 'Welcome to Vermont.'

Then he gazed at her gorgeous mother and brushed a light kiss on Anastasia's lips. "I missed you. Three days is a long time," he said.

Her alluring body moved closer to his. "I missed you, too."

He bent to the little girl's height. "Hello, Soo-Min. I've heard so much about you."

Soo-Min pushed oversized eyeglasses up her

nose and stared at him. "Your eyes are different from mine."

"Your eyes are prettier," he assured.

"Mommy said you're nice and tell funny jokes. Can you tell me one?"

"Age appropriate," Anastasia prompted.

He grinned and put a finger to his chin, pretending to ponder. "What did one tomato say to the other tomato?"

Soo-Min stopped jumping and attempted to balance on one foot. "I don't know, what?" She grabbed his hand to steady herself.

"You go ahead and I'll ketchup."

Her gurgle of laughter echoed in the parking garage as Anastasia guided them to her old Ford. He ducked into the passenger seat while Anastasia buckled Soo-Min into the back car seat.

"I hope your flight went well." Anastasia slipped into the driver's seat. "Did the board come to a decision regarding your software project?"

"They're considering a couple of other projects in the U.S. They'll let me know in a few days."

"I'm sure your schedule is packed. We're glad you made time for us." She slanted him a grin.

"Lonely and missing me?" His gaze slid meaningfully to her lips. "There's no place I'd rather be than here with you."

She flushed and drove down the ramp. "How long are you staying?"

"A few days, or until the investors come to a decision. Then I'll fly back to Charleston and return, hopefully, with Liz. I reminded her last night that you're anxious to file the petition."

"I thought she was in Las Vegas."

"We spoke on the phone." He looked at the clock on her dashboard. "I arranged for a car and rented a house while I'm here. I'll come by your apartment later this evening."

She gave him her address which he plugged into his phone.

"Then we can plan some fun activities with Soo-Min for the rest of the week," he added.

She eased the Ford into the left lane and picked up speed. "You haven't lived here for many years. Let me remind you that Stowe's population is still around five thousand people. Weekend excitement is a trip to a village shop for a cup of coffee or a visit to Stacy's Chocolatiers for a box of Sea Salt caramels." She gave a quick thumbs-up with one hand. "Although the Winter Carnival starts soon and is kid-friendly."

"You and I competed in a snow volleyball game at the Winter Carnival, remember? Guys versus girls."

She laughed. "And the girls won."

The girls won. And Anastasia had been exuberant with glee. She'd goaded him throughout the game with impertinent sidewise glances whenever he missed a shot, her smoky eyes ablaze with laughter. She'd been full of life and breathtaking. He'd wanted to take her in his arms even then.

As they sped past picturesque, snowy fields, he admired tree branches bowing under the heavy weight of snow. He'd forgotten how beautiful a winter scene in Vermont was. He rolled down the window a couple of inches and sniffed. Cold air whistled through the car, the scent frosty and exhilarating. Lovingly designed snowmen complete with carrot noses, short and tall, sat poignantly in every yard, a misshapen stick propped nearby. The desire to leap out of the car and make a dozen snowballs was number one on his 'to-do' list when they stopped.

"Soo-Min and I are preparing dinner tonight," Anastasia was saying. "You can expect kid's fare, which means macaroni and cheese and chicken fingers."

"I'll bring dessert." He turned to the backseat. "Soo-Min, what's your favorite dessert?"

"Chocolate ice cream!" Soo-Min declared. Then, she added, "Do you know The Wheels on the Bus song? I know every word of it. Want me to sing it to you all the way home?"

CHAPTER TWELVE

Soo-Min sat in the middle of Anastasia and Luciano on a park bench on Stowe's Main Street. Anastasia's cheeks tingled because of the freezing temperatures and her feet felt numb. She rubbed her gloved hands together and breathed into them, sending puffs of her warm breath into the air. Although she'd bundled her daughter in several layers of winter clothing, she still asked her, "Are you cold?"

Soo-Min licked traces of hot chocolate from her mouth and fanned at her face with mittened hands. "No, Mommy, I'm hot. And I'm squished because the zipper of my coat is choking my neck." She peered up at Luciano. "Can I sit on your lap?"

"No, honey," Anastasia began.

"That's all right. I like holding her." He lifted

Soo-Min onto his lap. "As long as I can take her picture first. Lean in, Anastasia. We'll take a selfie." She complied as he pulled out his phone and began singing, "Twinkle, twinkle, little butterfly ..."

Soo-Min giggled and Anastasia burst out laughing as his camera clicked.

"Ice carving demonstrations on Main Street are one of my favorite Winter Carnival events," Anastasia said after she'd wiped the tears of hilarity from her face. "I'm fascinated by the skill involved."

"Mommy, what ice sculpture are you voting for? I like the butterfly because it's a song." Soo-Min wiggled on Luciano's lap and gazed up at him. "What about you, Mr. Luciano? Will the butterfly fly away before we vote?"

He laughed and put his cell phone back in his coat pocket. "I think the butterfly is happy right where he is, just waiting for our vote so he can win."

Soo-Min let out a joyful squeal. "It's a she!"

"I knew that," he corrected himself.

Anastasia sat back and let the feelings of optimism surge through her. She loved Vermont. Thick snowflakes fell softly from the afternoon sky, and the little town would soon be covered by a fat white blanket.

Five days had flown by since Luciano had arrived, and he'd planned to return to Charleston in the morning. His investors had come to a decision, they'd informed him. Disarmingly calm, although an impending multi-million-dollar deal would greatly affect his billionaire status, he'd finalized the call with a professional 'thank you.'

He pointed to a run-down building across the way. "Isn't that my old boxing gym?"

"Yes, they went out of business several years ago."

He frowned. "That's too bad. Boxing kept so many guys off the streets and out of trouble. Any self-discipline I learned was taught at that gym. After hitting some punching bags, I'd feel physically and mentally exhausted when I got home."

"And all sweaty." She stared at the building, trying to drag her thoughts away from him leaving before she'd gotten her test results back from the lab. She'd hoped he'd insist on staying, declaring that the investors could wait because she was more important.

She needed his calm reassurance, his solid arm wrapped around her shoulders.

His gaze caught hers and he nodded, seeming to read her thoughts. "If the negotiations with my investors move along quickly, I'll return in a couple of days."

"You just want your birthday cake." She kept her tone light and avoided his eyes.

"I just want you, *Mia Cara*." His head dipped to kiss her. He, wearing a navy-blue parka and worn denim jeans, was recklessly handsome. They sat on the corner of Main Street, kissing with a passion that soon had her daughter giggling and pushing their faces apart.

"What about me, don't you want me?" Soo-Min asked.

Luciano bounced her on his lap and pressed a kiss on her forehead. "Of course I want you. Who wouldn't? And did you know I own a dog and her name is Lady?"

Soo-Min giggled and looked around. "Where is she?"

"My sister, Jaclyn, is watching the dog."

"I want to see your dog. What does she look like?"

"Well, she's big and has golden brown fur. She's a Golden Retriever." He pulled his phone out of his pocket. "Here's a picture."

Soo-Min stared intently at the photo. "I love Gold Treaters!"

"I do, too. She's an older dog, though, so I didn't want to take her on an airplane."

Soo-Min folded her tiny arms together. "I love dogs, and Mommy won't buy me one."

"I promise I'll bring Lady with me soon so you can meet her. Is that okay?"

With a nod, Soo-Min snuggled against his chest.

"Have you booked your flight back here?" Anastasia inquired.

"I'll book when I return to Charleston. Jaclyn

considered flying back with me, but she's been canoeing with her new instructor every day and seems preoccupied. Besides, she usually watches my dog when I'm away. I talked with Liz a number of times, and as soon as this Las Vegas case is wrapped up, she'll be able to come. Then we can file that petition."

He spoke so confidently, yet all Anastasia could think about was that he'd talked with Liz a number of times.

She looked away. A boulder settled where her optimism had previously surged. He might be spending every waking hour with her and Soo-Min, ice-skating and sledding, attending Broomball and hockey events at the ice arena, but he'd been free to talk all night with Liz.

"So, should we hold off on your birthday celebration so we can celebrate with Liz?" she snapped. "I can't fit thirty-five candles on one cake, by the way."

He seemed visibly taken aback by her churlishness. "Who said I wanted to share my birthday cake with anyone except you and Soo-Min?"

She fixed her gaze on a florist shop across the street, pondering whether or not he was telling the truth or just humoring her.

And why the answer meant so much.

"Look. We can see the house I'm renting from here." Luciano pointed past the florist and candy shop to a distant hill. "It's that little speck of a house at the very top."

Anastasia shaded her eyes from the rays of the setting sun. "The old Cobbo mansion? I didn't realize that home was vacant. The Cobbos used to boast about their 'expansive views of the Worcester mountains.' Isn't that mansion over seven thousand square feet?"

With a nod and a smile, he said, "Complete with a wood-fired pizza oven, a nine car garage and a large barn for horses, none of which I've used. The property is vacant, and the realtor said I could rent month to month until it sells. The view from the outdoor balcony is truly breathtaking."

But all she focused on was the 'renting month to month' observation, meaning he'd given thought to staying in Vermont after his birthday and for the filing of the custody petition.

"I'd love to see the property when you return. Your visit went by so quickly." She viewed the row of houses at the bottom of the hill where the lights were beginning to flicker from tiny windows as night settled in. Her vision blurred because of the snow falling on her eyelashes and she wiped at her eyes. Or perhaps it was because he was leaving and she felt a void she couldn't explain. "We should head back to my apartment. Soo-Min's enjoyed a very exciting day."

Luciano put a finger to his lips. "She's sleeping. I'll carry her to the car."

Carefully, he lifted Soo-Min from his lap and bundled her into his arms.

Soo-Min's eyes flew open. "Mommy, did the butterfly win?"

"They haven't announced the winners yet," Anastasia replied.

Soo-Min's small mittened fingers pointed to the park behind Luciano. "Can I play with the other kids?"

Anastasia shook her head. "Not today. It's getting dark and time for dinner."

Soo-Min tugged at the collar of Luciano's coat. "Do you know how to make snow angles?"

"Snow angels," Anastasia corrected.

"That's what I said, Mommy, snow angles. It's easy, Mr. Luciano. I can show you in my backyard while Mommy's cooking dinner."

CHAPTER THIRTEEN

*A*nastasia plunked her hands on her red-aproned hips and shook her head at the mess in her once neat kitchen. Now she knew why she'd given up cake decorating. Her gaze stopped at the mountainous heap of bowls and spatulas piled in the sink. Soo-Min stood on a chair at the kitchen table, a mixing bowl in one hand and large wooden spoon laden with butter cream frosting in the other.

"Mommy, this frosting is delicious!" She took another leisurely lick on the spoon. "Won't Mr. Luciano be happy when he sees our beautiful cake?"

Anastasia stood back from the table to admire their masterpiece. The heart-shaped, three-tiered vanilla cake sat proudly on a white pedestal stand. An empty jar of seedless strawberry jam sat on the table. Cherry-red decorative piping on the cake read, 'Happy Thirty-Fifth Birthday, Luciano.' As a garnish, Anastasia had added fresh strawberries and chocolate leaves on one side of the cake and dipped several strawberries in melted chocolate around the cake's border. On a whim, she'd added a pair of red boxing gloves, shaped like mittens, below the piping.

Her kitchen clock chimed four o'clock. Luciano had called the previous morning, assuring her that he'd arrive in plenty of time to celebrate his birthday. He'd sounded rushed and preoccupied, the same way he'd sounded every day on the phone since returning to Charleston, answering her inquiries regarding his meetings with clipped, short replies.

Suppose he was too busy and didn't show?

No. He'd never disappoint her and Soo-Min, especially on Valentine's Day.

Although, she thought wistfully, throughout the day she'd half-expected the florist to ring the doorbell of her apartment holding a bouquet of flowers from Luciano, along with a tender note written in his bold handwriting, assuring her that he was counting the minutes until he saw her again.

No flowers had arrived. Certainly, no note.

It was his birthday, not hers, she chided herself. She pulled off her apron and kissed her daughter's sticky chin, envisioning his lazy smile when he strode into the kitchen and viewed his birthday cake, ablaze with candles. She'd purchased a small red leather journal for his birthday gift. After nibbling on the end of her pen for several minutes while she'd considered what was in her heart, she'd written inside the front cover: '*Che Sara Sara.*'

Whatever will be, will be, she mused, because the future wasn't theirs to see.

Below the Italian song lyrics she'd added, 'Your future will be magnificent. I hope you'll fill this journal with wonderful memories in the coming years.'

She paused, envisioning him as a brave little Italian boy with disheveled brown hair and a pensive, penetrating gaze, clutching his birth mother's journal, his only memento of her. What had been his thoughts, his fears when he traveled to America? How frightening it must've been for him to step onto a foreign country with so many different sights and smells assaulting him all at once. Her heart swelled with pride at the principled, successful man he'd become.

"Tonight's going to be perfect, honey," she declared to Soo-Min.

"Every day is perfect with you, Mommy!" Soo-Min giggled.

Anastasia dabbed at her eyes with her apron. Her daughter knew just what to say to chase away any doubts. Of course he'd arrive. He was a millionaire and had projects and employees and business ventures, all vying for his attention. *Be understanding.*

Anastasia lifted her daughter down from the

kitchen chair. "Let's get you in the bathtub so you'll look beautiful for Luciano."

"I'm not wearing that lace dress you bought. It's too itchy."

Anastasia laughed. "You can pick out whatever you want to wear tonight, as long as it's red."

"Why?"

"It's Valentine's Day."

"Are you wearing red?"

"Yes." Anastasia had bought a lace dress. It was clingy and shorter than she usually wore, a crimson lace sheath lined in satin and with an open back. She'd splurged on a pair of black lace-up stilettos and planned on pulling her hair back in a messy bun. She grinned, thinking about his seductive perusal and approving smile when he arrived.

*E*xcept he never showed.

Anastasia sat with her daughter on their worn living room couch. Between them, they'd eaten almost half the birthday cake, although Anastasia had eaten the most.

"Mommy, we never finished blowing up the balloons, and there's a red and a white one left." Soo-Min sat on the couch swinging her legs, then somersaulted across the living room floor, her chubby legs clad in patterned tights, her feet facing upward as she attempted a head stand. She'd decided to wear a dress after all, adorned with sequins along the sleeves and a crinoline petticoat underneath.

"It's after eleven o'clock and well past your bedtime." Anastasia unlaced her stilettos and flung them off. "You've had way too much sugar." She changed her daughter into a pair of warm pajamas. After teeth-brushing, she tucked her into bed. The bath and hair wash could wait until morning.

Anastasia's inner voice chattered in her ear, reminding that she'd failed the perfect mother award today.

For the past several hours, she'd constantly checked her cell phone, waiting for a text message or phone call from Luciano. But he hadn't bothered to contact her.

More than once, she'd been tempted to call him. She'd even checked her email for his flight numbers, realizing that he'd never sent her that information. Usually he was so meticulous, with each day of his life completely planned.

But not today.

After reading the barnyard animals book to Soo-Min, her daughter imitated the sound of a bleating lamb for the tenth time, petted the soft fuzzy fur in the book and fell asleep.

The clock in the kitchen chimed midnight. Valentine's Day was officially over.

Anastasia padded to her bedroom and sat on the bed. Hesitating at first, she slowly punched in Jaclyn's phone number, mentally rehearsing what she'd say. She didn't want to alarm Jaclyn, but it was normal to be concerned about Luciano, right?

Jaclyn's phone rang several times, then went to voice mail. Her recorded voice declared, "Today's Valentine's Day and the best day to book a cruise. You may be here, but I'll take you there. Leave a message."

In the background of the recording, a dog barked, sounding suspiciously like Lady.

So where was Luciano?

Anastasia clicked the end button. She didn't leave a message.

CHAPTER FOURTEEN

*A*nastasia jerked up from a jumbled dream to the sound of an insistently ringing cell phone. She stared at the time, astonished that she'd slept until eight o'clock in the morning. Even more surprising, her daughter's room was quiet and she was apparently still asleep.

"Hello?" Anastasia answered.

"Dr. Bon's office calling for Anastasia Markow," responded an efficient sounding nurse. "Your lab report came back and Dr. Bon would like to see you in his office today."

"Can ... Can you share the results with me?" Anastasia asked slowly.

"I'm sorry, that's not allowed. However, Dr. Bon will explain everything. The earliest appointment is eleven o'clock this morning."

"I see, and thank you. Eleven is fine." Anastasia clicked the end button.

Appointment. Dr. Bon. She stared at her bandaged wrist, the conversation hitting her hard. It was bad news, or the doctor's office wouldn't have scheduled an appointment so quickly. The thought was like a crushing weight on her chest, and she grabbed the bedpost as she stood, staggering to her feet. She'd be facing her doctor's appointment alone. Again.

She expelled a long, drawn-out breath. For the first time in her life, she'd half-believed that a man really had cared about her and that Luciano was more than a childhood friend and ally. Somehow, she'd believed he'd offered love and support, but those were the daydreams of a giddy, foolish school-girl. *Pathetic.*

She lifted her chin. *No. Not this time.*

She made a hasty call to Justin and Eliza, who both assured her that Soo-Min would be well taken care of and encouraged Anastasia to take all the time she needed.

She felt a twinge of guilt for what she did next, because she dialed Liz's office in Charleston.

The secretary with the brisk voice answered. "Fullman law offices."

Anastasia felt her hands start to sweat. "This is Anastasia Markow. Liz Fullman is arranging a trip to Vermont regarding a custody filing. Is she back in town from Las Vegas?"

The secretary hesitated. "Ms. Fullman is out of the country. Let me check your file." The secretary stepped away from the phone for several minutes. Returning, she said with polite indifference, "Ms. Fullman is sending Miss Debbie Porter, one of our junior associates, to Vermont. When the associate arrives in a few days, she'll contact you to arrange a time to meet at the Family Court Clerk's Office in Hyde Park."

With a 'thank you,' Anastasia walked to her daughter's bedroom. Soo-Min sat on her bed with a pillow propped behind her head. She was reading the barnyard animals book aloud, mimicking the sounds of the animals.

"You'll be going to your father's house today." Anastasia opened the painstakingly neat dresser drawer to pull out a pair of corduroy pants and matching unicorn top for her daughter.

Soo-Min jumped off the bed and clapped her hands. "Yay! It's fun at Daddy's house. He throws a ball with me inside, Mommy, in the living room, and Eliza never gets mad about the mess."

"Oh," Anastasia answered quietly. Perhaps Justin and Eliza were better parents than she realized. Soo-Min seemed happy and content whenever she visited them. She came back clean and well-fed, filled with stories of her adventures. Sure, they allowed her to stay up late sometimes, although hadn't Anastasia done the same thing last night?

But Soo-Min ... Soo-Min was her daughter, the child she'd waited for all those endless years of infertility treatments. At thirty-two years old, she'd promised herself that Soo-Min deserved to have the best. The best mother, care, parenting. Nonetheless, that image of her daughter laughing and clapping her hands, excited to go to her father's house, played continuously in Anastasia's mind.

She let out a breath she hadn't realized she was holding as she dressed. Perhaps she was wrong. Perhaps Soo-Min needed her parents to work together.

Several hours later, Anastasia sat on a heavy wooden chair in Dr. Bon's office.

"The diagnosis of melanoma has been confirmed," Dr. Bon began, sitting across from her at his desk. "I suspected as much because the tumor was cracked and bleeding. However, it's in the early stages. I'll order blood work and, assuming the results show no traces of melanoma in any organs, I'll schedule surgery to remove the tumor and surrounding tissues."

She took a deep breath. "And then?"

He smiled reassuringly. "And then no other treatment is needed."

"Thank you." Her cell phone pinged and she reached inside her purse. "I'm sorry. I thought I'd left my phone on vibrate. I won't be long. The message might be about my daughter."

Dr. Bon pushed back his chair and readied himself to leave. "Take all the time you need. My office will call you with details of the surgery date." He left the office and kept the door ajar.

She opened her phone to a text and photo from Luciano:

'Buona Sera, Mia Cara, I'm in Italy! I found my Italian family and can't wait for you and Soo-Min to meet them. I'm in a little town in northwestern Sicily and staring out at the Egadi Islands as I type this, although it's getting dark because it's nearing six o'clock. My Nona, the woman with the white streak in her gray hair, is standing beside me. My great-aunt is the lady wearing the funny straw hat. And they said I have a birth sister and that she was adopted as a baby. Her name is Clara and she lives in Ireland. I have so much to tell you. I will call as soon as I get a good cell phone connection. I miss you and Soo-Min. *Arrivederci.'*

In the photo, Luciano sat at the bottom of a broad band of stone steps flanked by rugged mountains on one side and a distant, sandy seashore on the other. He was smiling broadly, holding a stem of fresh basil. He was surrounded by several dark-haired children and his Nona and great-aunt stood beside him. In the far corner, just beyond the steps, a breathtaking blonde woman was laughing into the camera.

Liz.

Anastasia's hands closed around the arm rails of the chair, a lump of sadness lodged in her throat. Luciano was in Italy. With Liz.

CHAPTER FIFTEEN

Anastasia drove directly to the familiar school where she'd taught several years before. She walked to the office, surprised by the pert, new secretary with curly auburn hair sitting behind a computer with her hand on the mouse. The previous secretary must've retired. Anastasia noted that the auburn-haired secretary was surfing the internet and was about to purchase some new makeup.

"Is Mrs. Danner available?" Anastasia asked.

The secretary shook her head. "Mrs. Danner hasn't been the principal here for a couple of years."

"Can I speak to the new principal?

"Mr. Norr? Sorry. He won't be in until next week. Would you like to make an appointment to see him?"

"Yes, and I'd like to fill out an application for a

teacher position. I'm certified in grades Kindergarten through sixth grade. I used to teach here."

The secretary took her hand off the mouse and minimized the computer screen. "All the applications are submitted online. There hasn't been any new hires for a couple of years, though, because of state cutbacks."

"Thank you."

There were other schools, Anastasia told herself encouragingly, as she walked back to her car. She could apply to every school in the district online, which was much more convenient.

Nevertheless, to return to her apartment in order to begin submitting, she'd need to drive. And she couldn't muster up the strength to put her key into the ignition. She sat in her old Ford in the parking lot, staring at a run-down school she hardly recognized.

Her cell phone vibrated. She recognized the Charleston area code, although the caller ID identified the number to 'Liz Fullman.'

"Yes?" Anastasia answered.

"*Mia Cara*, finally, I have decent cell phone service. Did you get my text and photo? You didn't respond."

She swallowed, feeling her heart beat triple time. "When did you arrive in Italy?"

"My investigators contacted me by email when I got back in Charleston. Then they called and said they'd found a solid lead and I needed to leave immediately for Italy. It happened very fast."

"Why didn't you call? I waited ... waited ..." Angrily, she swiped tears from her cheeks and covered the phone with her hand so he wouldn't hear her choking up.

"Did you get your lab results?"

"Yes." Her fingers trembled as she held the phone. "It's melanoma."

There was a hesitation on the line. "What's next?"

She leaned weakly against the car's seat. "The same procedure as last time."

"We will get through it together."

How? From Italy? She shook her head. She didn't state her reservations aloud.

"*Mia Cara*, are you there? Italy is exactly how I remembered— *bella,* the sky, the sunshine, the fig trees. You and Soo-Min will love it."

Except they'd never see it.

"We baked a cake for your birthday." *And Valentine's Day.* "Then we waited all night for you to arrive."

"I'm sorry. I spent my birthday in a jet-lagged haze. This flight takes over fifteen hours counting the layovers."

She inhaled, then spoke sharply. "So Liz flew to Italy with you?"

The silence of the next few moments was interrupted by static. "She dropped all her appointments to come with me. She's leaving Italy today and flying back to Vegas."

"How long are you staying?"

"Another week, perhaps. There are some cousins I haven't met who live in a neighboring town."

"I'm happy for you." She pressed the phone close to her ear, holding it so tightly her fingers cramped. Then she took a long, suffocated breath. "Please, Luciano, don't call me again."

"What? What did you say?" The phone crackled. Luciano's voice was a static blur and the connection ended.

CHAPTER SIXTEEN

*Y*ou're acting ridiculous," Jaclyn scolded over the speaker phone as Anastasia drove to the Family Court Clerk's Office in Hyde Park a few days afterward. Liz's junior associate, Debbie Porter, had arranged a ten o'clock meeting to assist Anastasia with the custody petition filing.

Anastasia's insides had cringed when she'd asked Justin and Eliza to take care of Soo-Min. Her explanation had been vague and she'd mumbled something about checking out neighboring counties for a teaching job. Although if she were honest with herself, she was being deceitful to a man who may not have loved her anymore, but who was proving to be a good father.

Anastasia huffed into the phone. "Luciano left

without a word. No phone call, no text, nothing. Soo-Min and I baked the most beautiful cake for his Valentine birthday."

"So bake another cake."

"It's too late, his birthday's over. Valentine's Day is over. He could've called from the airport before he boarded the plane. This was such an important time in his life, finding and meeting his Italian relatives."

"And you wanted to share that moment with him."

"Is that so wrong?"

"Can't you be happy for him? There'll be other moments. He didn't have time," Jaclyn said. "His secretary said he received a phone call during the board meeting, answered the call, and then got up and left the meeting with no explanation. He asked her to call me to watch Lady with an abrupt explanation of where he was headed, and then he was gone."

Anastasia drew a ragged breath. If she said the words aloud, they'd become a fact. "Liz is with him in Italy, isn't she?" She wanted to add that it didn't matter in the least. Instead, she said nothing.

A brief beat ticked by. "They're friends, nothing more, although she'd certainly welcome his advances. His secretary said that Liz had just gotten back from Vegas and stopped in his office when he received the call from the investigator. She had her bags packed from Vegas and insisted on going with him."

'What about me?' Anastasia rubbed the back of her neck, remembering her daughter's adamant voice. She was starting to act exactly like Soo-Min, as if she were a four-year-old child.

He'd pressed a kiss on Soo-Min's forehead. *"Of course I want you. Who wouldn't?"*

But nobody wants you, Anastasia, an inner voice whispered. Not your mother, not your ex-husband. No one loves you. She squeezed her eyes shut for a second. *Luciano, I thought you were starting to love me.*

Jaclyn sighed impatiently. "The main reason I called was to ask about your mole. What did the lab results show? Did you call your aunt and uncle and let them know?"

"It's melanoma and no, not yet."

"Anastasia, I'm so sorry." A pause. "What's next?"

"Dr. Bonn said the surgery will be minimal, same as last time."

"Not so bad."

"Not so bad," Anastasia echoed, driving up to a large brick building. "I'm in Hyde Park and there's a very pretty young woman with long blonde hair waiting outside the Clerk's Office. She's probably Debbie, the junior associate."

"Call me when you're done filing that petition," Jaclyn said. "Although, honestly, this custody pro-ceeding is going to be emotionally and physically draining for everyone. The more you told me about what your aunt and uncle had said, the more I'm agreeing with them. Okay, so Justin's a jerk, but it doesn't matter if he's a good father. And Soo-Min seems to enjoy Eliza. Do you really want to upset your daughter with home studies and arguments and disruptions?"

Anastasia parked the car. Her chest tightened with an aching lump of contrition. "I'm not so sure anymore."

"Well, it's your decision. And by the way, you haven't asked about my canoeing lessons with Bart."

"Apparently Sam isn't on your eligible bachelor radar anymore?" Anastasia looked in the mirror and gave her friend a long-distance grin. "I hope Bart's rich because you love a lavish lifestyle."

"He's as poor as a church mouse, as the saying goes. Although now I realize that love is all you need. Not money, not prestige, not a great job and expensive home. Just love and a canoe."

"I'm assuming your Valentine's Day went better than mine."

"Bart looks at me the way Luciano looks at you. I've watched my brother, and he's in love with you. And you love him, right? You always have."

"It's hard to get over being hurt."

"I'm the first person to let my brother know when he's done something wrong, but he'll make it up to you. I know him. He didn't mean to hurt you."

"I thought I knew him, too," Anastasia whispered, clicking off the phone. She ducked out of the car and walked toward the Family Court Clerk's Office.

She'd traveled to Charleston for information to file for sole custody of Soo-Min. Sure, it'd been wonderful to see Luciano again and renew their friendship. However, she hadn't been looking for romance.

Why then, couldn't she stop visualizing him laughing while making snow angels, 'snow angles' according to Soo-Min, in her tiny backyard? And why couldn't she forget his grinning rendition of 'Hark the Herald Angles Sing,' sung in his deep, baritone voice?

She'd joined in the chorus, laughing uproariously, so hard that tears had run down their cheeks. She remembered her daughter's endless giggles, and how the creases on Luciano's forehead had disappeared the entire time he'd been in Vermont.

Funny, she hadn't thought about that until now.

But now was too late. Because now it was over.

CHAPTER SEVENTEEN

"Hi, are you Anastasia Markow? I'm Debbie Porter, a junior associate at the Fullman Law Offices."

Anastasia extended her hand, surprised to feel the young woman's sweaty palm. "Yes, I'm pleased to meet you."

"Ms. Liz Fullman sent me, as you know." The associate looked around. "Where's your ex-husband? What's his name again?"

"Justin. I wasn't aware he was supposed to be here. No one told me."

The associate frowned and scratched her head. "I'm not really sure, either."

Anastasia dropped her hand and bristled. "Shouldn't that be something you'd know?"

"I was assigned this case a couple of days ago.

Ms. Fullman mentioned being obligated to do a quick favor for someone. All the case files are backed up because of the Charleston storm and all the other lawyers in the Fullman offices are overloaded."

Anastasia struggled with her impatience and began walking toward the doorway. "Shall we go inside, introduce ourselves and get started?"

The associate stared at Anastasia with a look resembling stage fright and stopped mid-step. "Actually, this is my first case, and I don't want to make a fool of myself. This could have devastating consequences on my career."

Second by second, Anastasia felt any confidence she'd had left filtering away, but she could do this on her own. She'd promised herself she wouldn't rely on anyone. She turned to the associate. "I don't need your help."

"Really? Are you sure?" The associate looked so relieved that Anastasia almost wanted to put her arms around her to offer reassurance.

Anastasia nodded. "I'm sure. Thanks for coming, and sorry that Liz sent you all this way for apparently nothing."

The young girl offered a hopeful smile. "I can make the one o'clock flight back to Charleston if I leave now."

"Then you should go." Anastasia stood in the doorway of the clerk's office and watched the associate hurry back to her car and drive off. She paused with her hand on the door handle and gazed inside the office without going inside.

A woman from the office came to the door and opened it. "May I help you?"

Anastasia hesitated, just for a moment, and shook her head. "No. I thought I needed something here. I was mistaken."

She walked to her car with her shoulders erect and drove to Justin's house. Eliza and Soo-Min were playing cards on the living room floor. Justin was in the kitchen, watching a TV Food channel, and the chef was explaining the proper way to make sticky rice.

"How's your day going?" Justin asked.

She met her ex's smile with an open nod. "Everything's better now. What about you?"

"I'm enjoying my week off from work. There are advantages to a professor's schedule."

"Mommy," Soo-Min called from the living room, "can I spend the night at Daddy's house? We're going to wrap seaweed around the rice Daddy's cooking. It sounds yucky, but it's really good. Eliza said it's from Korea."

Anastasia laughed. "Yes, of course you can spend the night, honey." She walked to the living room and sat on the floor. "Thanks for everything, Eliza. I know how much you care about Soo-Min. I'm sorry I've been so critical in the past."

"Apology accepted." Eliza pushed a pale blonde streak of hair from her face. "It isn't easy striving to meet your high standards, although I try my best. We hadn't expected you home for another few days, so if you need the time to prepare for your surgery or submit job applications, we're fine with that."

"We'll save some seaweed for you, Mommy. Eliza taught me how to do cartwheels. Wanna see?" Soo-Min pushed her cards aside and demonstrated two flawless cartwheels across the living room.

Anastasia, Justin, and Eliza clapped in unison.

"Thanks, I could use the next several days to submit teacher applications. I'll take Soo-Min to the last day of the Winter Carnival at the end of week," Anastasia said. "They'll be announcing the winners of the ice sculpting competition."

"No problem," Justin said.

And there it was. Parents talking with each other, without the courts involved, doing what was in the best interests of their child.

Anastasia smiled at Justin and Eliza and whispered, "Let's hope the butterfly sculpture wins or I'll be dashing off Main Street and straight back to your house with a very unhappy little girl."

CHAPTER EIGHTEEN

*W*inter in Vermont was a season that lasted for months, although every day in February seemed a little brighter and closer to spring.

Anastasia stood in the playground, pushing Soo-Min on a 'big girl' swing. The weather had warmed, and tiny blades of grass pushed through the thawing snow.

"Higher, Mommy, higher!" her daughter exclaimed. Soo-Min turned to another little girl swinging next to her. "I want to swing as high as Justine. She's my new friend and goes to my school."

Anastasia grinned at Justine's mother. They'd exchanged phone numbers to set up play dates for the girls.

"You don't need to stand here while the girls

swing. I can handle both munchkins," Justine's mother said.

"Are you sure?" Anastasia asked. "I'd love a cup of coffee."

"Go ahead. I guarantee we'll still be here in twenty minutes."

Grabbing her hot coffee a few minutes later, Anastasia found a bench near the back of the park where she could see her daughter and new friend swinging.

She sipped and smiled, comfortable with her custody decision. She'd made peace with herself, and peace with Justin and Eliza. She'd been jealous and admittedly bitter of Justin's happiness with Eliza, and she wasn't proud to acknowledge those traits in herself.

She half-sighed. Her face burned with memories of how she'd spoken to Eliza on several occasions— judgmental and dismissive of the young woman's parenting skills. Her apology to Eliza had been long overdue and had been graciously accepted.

That morning, Anastasia's aunt and uncle had been encouraging and understanding during their phone exchange.

"If your prior school doesn't have any teaching vacancies, apply at others," Uncle Filipp had instructed. "You're a smart and determined young woman."

"Actually," she'd replied, "there's a job opening

for a second grade teacher in a nearby district that I hadn't considered until I looked online. If I get the job, Soo-Min can attend Kindergarten there, so we'll both be at the same school."

"Sounds good, dear. And how is Luciano, your handsome billionaire friend?" her aunt had asked.

At the mention of his name, Anastasia's lips had quivered, and she'd closed her eyes for a moment to hold back the bleakness filling her chest.

"I believe he's in Italy," she'd answered vaguely.

"He'll be back," her aunt had assured.

Although he wouldn't be back, because he'd finally found what he'd been looking for in Italy. His heritage. His birth family. And with the elegant, successful Liz by his side.

With an audible sigh, Anastasia's gaze shifted restlessly to the crowd of people filling the park, apparently waiting for the ice competition's results. The weather was turning blustery, and she took a last sip of coffee, then folded up the collar of her scarlet wool jacket.

She'd lived in this little town her entire life. It was her home. But today, despite her daughter's laughing shouts coming from the nearby swings, the festive scents of outdoor barbecue and hot chocolate in the air, she felt lonely and forlorn.

She set her empty cup on the bench, opened her large purse and pulled out the small, red journal she'd bought for his birthday gift. She'd decided to keep it with her, keeping a log of her daily activities. So far, she hadn't written a word.

She fingered the smooth leather. '*Che Sara Sara*, whatever will be, will be,' she'd written. A special gift, a special Valentine. She'd assumed Luciano had been on a plane flying to Vermont while she and Soo-Min were baking his birthday cake, although in reality he'd been flying to Italy, his birthplace, with Liz.

Anastasia furiously swiped away the tears streaming down her cheeks and placed the journal back in her purse. Her grip on her feelings was apparently tenuous when it came to Luciano.

No more thinking, she told herself sternly. But her mind wasn't listening, continuing to batter her emotions with replays:

The first time they'd met, he'd returned home from a boxing match, his chin bruised, holding a bag of ice on his swollen, bloody nose. He'd shrugged off her worried teenage exclamations. Never had he looked more handsome, or more vulnerable. Her beat-up, non-swimming Greek god. As she'd predicted that day, his nose, indeed, had been broken.

And sixteen years later, sitting in his luxurious Charleston mansion:

"Our lives are made up of different chapters," he'd said solemnly. *"You seem to be in the middle of a rough one."*

Briefly, she squeezed her eyes closed and leaned back against the cold bench. She must bring her emotions in check. Sure, she'd once been a giddy schoolgirl with a mad crush on a man who's always been out of reach. But not anymore. Today was the conclusion of this rough chapter of her life.

"Mommy, you're not listening." Dimly, her mind registered that Soo-Min was tugging at her sleeve.

Anastasia bent her head. "I'm sorry, honey, what did you say?"

Soo-Min pointed toward Main Street, an impish smile glowing in her eyes. "I said that dog looks like Mr. Luciano's Gold Treater."

Anastasia slowly stood, staring at the tall, muscular man walking along Main Street, firmly holding a Golden Retriever's leash in one hand, and a large brown bag emblazoned with 'Stacy Chocolatiers' in the other. The man seemed to be searching for someone, his gaze drifting past the barbecue and hot chocolate stands, past the butterfly ice sculpture. Anastasia's heart pounded as his brown-eyed gaze looked directly into hers.

She blinked. Her feet seemed rooted in place. She wanted to tear her gaze away and look somewhere else, anywhere else, although his penetrating gaze wouldn't allow it.

He looked tanned, a black bristled beard along his strong jaw. He strode quickly toward her, jostling through the crowd, holding her gaze, remorse and desperation etched on his masculine face.

"Mr. Luciano. Mommy, that's him!" Soo-Min

grabbed Anastasia's hand and yanked her forward, wending their way around groups of children and parents. "Hurry, Mommy, you're moving too slow!"

A moment later, they stood a few inches apart.

Anastasia found herself breathing heavily, trying to collect herself.

"Anastasia," he said in a beloved, familiar voice, "I've missed you so much." The sincerity in his tone sent a trembling up and down her body. He handed her the large brown bag. "These are for you."

Inside were a dozen red foil boxes of Sea Salt caramels.

"Thank ... thank you. How ... how did you know they're my favorite candy?"

"I know you as well as I know myself." He shrugged in that endearingly boyish way of his and drew her to him, gently sliding his arm around her. "I would've bought more but—"

She shook her head and moved closer to him. "It'll take me a year to eat these, and my daughter will never go to sleep from being on a sugar high."

"Good. We can stay awake at night and watch the Worcester mountains from the top of the hill."

"How will we be able to do that? You don't live —" She stopped in mid-sentence and moved back a step. "What hill?"

"Mr. Luciano!" Her daughter petted the dog. "I saw Gold Treater first. And I love candy!"

Luciano bent down. "I've missed you, Soo-Min."

"And I love your dog!" The dog wagged its tail and nuzzled against Soo-Min. "Can I hold his leash while you and Mommy kiss?"

Luciano grinned. "Lady's a she. And yes, you can hold her leash while your mother and I kiss." He stood and wrapped both arms around Anastasia. "We have your daughter's permission."

She hesitated. "How long have you been back from Italy?"

"Speaker phones are a brilliant invention." He pressed her tighter to his strong form. "How long does it take to fly eighteen hours with two layovers, buy a new Hummer, a house, a business, then drive to Stowe from Charleston?"

Her heart skipped a beat. "Twenty four hours?"

"Give or take twelve hours, considering Lady needs walking every few hours during a car ride."

"You bought the Cobbo mansion?"

"It's the perfect house for a guy like me because there's no ocean in sight." He gave her one of his lazy smiles, and his hands slid possessively up her back. "Can I show you how much I missed you?" He didn't wait for permission. His lips came down on hers.

Sighing, she twined her hands around his neck and the kiss deepened.

Soo-Min jumped up and down. "Mommy, can you hold Lady's leash? I want to play with my friend by the monkey bars." She glanced at the dog. "Sorry,

Mr. Luciano, but Lady rolled in the snow and got all muddy."

Anastasia broke the kiss and grabbed the leash from Soo-Min. "Go ahead, honey. We can see you from here."

"Your daughter has the opposite of perfect timing," Luciano wryly remarked. He rested his chin on her head. "Don't ever leave me again," he whispered.

She tilted her head up. "You left me."

"I'm sorry. I needed to act quickly. My heritage search has been so elusive with many false leads and dead ends. However, one of the thirty investigators I'd hired was certain he'd found my birth family."

She rubbed her hand against his bristled jaw. "You don't need to explain or apologize. I understand how much this search meant to you."

"Come to Italy with me this summer. You and Soo-Min?" He looked down, apparently to ensure that Anastasia had nodded. "I bought a villa in a tiny Italian mountain town, and you'll love my birth family. They're loud and funny and content with very little. I offered to buy them whatever they wanted, although they refused. They said that my returning to the town, and knowing I was okay, was the greatest gift ..." He cleared his throat.

"And you have a sister in Ireland?" she prompted.

He nodded. "My younger sister, Clara. I vaguely remember a baby in my family's apartment in Italy, before my mother got sick. Clara was placed in the

Italian orphanage soon after I was, although I never knew it."

She smiled up into his beloved face. "Sounds like I better update my passport."

He laughed. "First, will you and your daughter come for a ride with me? I have a surprise for you."

A few minutes later, they retrieved Soo-Min from the monkey bars and piled into his Hummer, following a road leading to the Cobbo mansion. The sun was dipping lower in the sky as Luciano parked near the entrance of the sprawling estate. With the dog trotting by his side, he led them across the driveway. "I read a funny joke while I was on the plane," he said with a wink. "Want to hear it?"

Anastasia couldn't help a smirk of helpless amusement. "Go ahead."

"Why did the billionaire leave his oceanside mansion?" he asked.

"I'm sure you'll tell me."

He tried to keep a straight face and ended up grinning. "The mansion was too current."

"That is so *not* funny!" She gave a bark of laughter anyway and Soo-Min twirled and chuckled.

They crossed a wide front porch to a triple wooden door fixed with double brass handles. "Remember I said this was a surprise?" He covered her and Soo-Min's eyes with his hands, clicked open the door and ushered them inside.

"Ready?"

She nodded. Soo-Min giggled.

He dropped his hands. The large living room overflowed with hundreds of candy-red roses, the light, fragrant scent filling the expansive living room. Crystal vases filled with white roses lined the expansive staircase.

She gasped. Soo-Min squealed with delight. The muddy dog barked and bounded for a pristine white couch.

"I wasn't sure if you liked red or white roses." he explained. "I wanted to send them to you for Valentine's Day, but because of the travel and time difference, I lost track of the days."

Tears filled her eyes. "They're beautiful!"

"Mommy, I'm going to sniff every single rose," Soo-Min declared, dipping her nose into each bouquet as she began circling the room.

Luciano drew Anastasia into his embrace. She looked away, uncertain of meeting his gaze.

"What is it?" he prodded.

"It's too much, the candy, the roses—"

"You wouldn't want to deprive me of giving you gifts?" He smiled and chucked her chin. "You know I love beautiful things."

She rubbed the back of her neck and her gaze swept downcast. "I know."

"Then what is it?" he prodded.

She didn't want to ask, although she needed to, because otherwise the hurt and jealousy she harbored would spread and put a wedge in their relationship.

"It's Liz," she said quietly.

"I heard her assistant wasn't much help filing the custody case."

"No help at all. However, in the end it was for the best because I've decided not to file. Justin and Eliza care about Soo-Min as much as I do, and everyone was right; it's in my daughter's best interests to have a good relationship with them."

He tightened his hold and lightly kissed her. "And Liz is a friend, only a friend, who didn't like Italy, by the way. Once we arrived, she didn't venture within five miles of my birth town, declaring the entire town decrepit, old, and utterly boring. She's pursuing that movie star nobody's heard of and happily headed back to Vegas."

Anastasia smiled with a mixture of relief and happiness.

"Mommy, Lady and I are gonna race up and down the stairs. Wanna watch us?" Soo-Min asked.

A vase filled with roses and water toppled as Soo-Min and Lady sped past.

"They'll make a mess of your beautiful home in no time," Anastasia predicted.

Luciano shrugged. "I hired a small staff, including a housecleaner, horse handler and stable keeper. Can Soo-Min help me select a couple of ponies tomorrow? I researched and Welsh ponies are a good choice for small children."

Laughter quivered on Anastasia's lips. "I'm sure she'll love lending her expertise."

*H*ours later, they sat together on the living room floor. The sun had set and a warm fire burned in the fireplace. Luciano gazed down at his beautiful wife-to-be. She'd been quiet for several minutes, snuggled in his lap.

Soo-Min snored softly on the couch, an 'I Love Vermont' blanket bundled around her. She kept one arm firmly around a devoted Lady stretched out beside her.

Luciano brushed a strand of hair from Anastasia's temple. "Are you sleeping?" he murmured.

She snuggled a laugh into his chest, then turned her face up to his. "Not anymore."

He pressed his lips to her forehead. "There is much I need to explain."

She leaned back. "Beginning with Italy? I understand if you feel your real home is there." Her voice shook slightly as she spoke.

"I believed that the only place I truly belonged was Italy, and discovered I was wrong. Sure, my ethnic identity was fractured, and I blamed everyone except myself, although any barriers I put up were within me. My adoptive parents gave me food, shelter, and most importantly, love. Without their support, I wouldn't have been able to accomplish everything I've done." He gazed into her smoky blue-gray eyes. "What I'm saying is that my home is here, and I want to live life with you and your beautiful daughter. That is, if you'll have an opinionated, dead-wrong guy for a husband."

Her eyes glistened with tears. The room filled with silence.

"Will you marry me?" he asked.

She nodded.

He framed her face in his hands. Her tousled hair tumbled over her shoulders. "Say it out loud. I've waited sixteen years."

"Yes, yes, of course!" She flung herself against him for an endless, breathless kiss. Then she drew back and stood quickly. "You've given me so much, and I also have a gift for you." She retrieved her purse and pulled out a small red journal. With an enchanting smile, she handed it to him. "Happy thirty-fifth birthday."

He leafed through the pages in a surreal sense of wonder. "How did you know what this would mean to me?"

Her voice was tender, yet serious. "I know you as well as I know myself." She echoed his earlier words.

He read the inside cover aloud. "*Che Sara Sara*,"

then changed the wording. "*Our* magnificent future is ours to see." He wanted to tell her how much she and Soo-Min meant to him. He was only able to whisper, "Thank you," before bending his head to kiss her.

A while later, he stood to light several candles and placed them on the mantel. Then they both stretched their legs out on the carpet, propping pillows against the couch so that they could lean against it.

"What about your business?" Anastasia asked, half to herself.

"I can run my business from here."

"But you're giving up so much. Your beautiful Charleston office, for one."

He shrugged and his lips twitched. "A billionaire can do whatever he wants."

She regarded him with a questioning expression. "Your negotiations went well?"

He smiled, confirming, "The investors liked my software project."

"What about Jaclyn?"

"She moved in with her canoe instructor while her bungalow is being renovated. I'm sure they'll visit us."

Tears came down Anastasia's cheeks. His arms automatically encircled her as she turned her body closer to his.

"I'll stop crying in a minute, I promise." She

sniffed and regarded him with a rueful gaze. "It's just that I'm so happy and love you so much."

He shook his head and silenced her tears with a kiss. "But I love you more."

HE END

A NOTE FROM JOSIE

Dear Friends,

Thank you for reading I Love You More. This book is available in ebook, Paperback, Large Print Paperback, and Audiobook.

If you loved this sweet Valentine romance as much as I loved writing it, please help other people find *I Love You More* by posting your amazing review here.

I'd love to meet you in person someday, but in the meantime, all I can offer is a sincere and grateful thank you. Without your support, my books would not be possible.

As I write my next sweet or inspirational romance, remember this: Have you ever tried something you were afraid to try because it mattered so much to you? I did, when I started writing. Take the chance, and just do something you love.

My Spotify Play List for I Love You More is here.

With sincere appreciation for your support,
Josie Riviera

P.S. Thousands of families around the world have opened their homes and hearts through international adoption. Soo-Min is the embodiment of many, many fortunate adoptive children and parents who've together created forever families.

Josie Riviera
    Want more sweet Valentine romances?
    Check out:

1-800-CUPID
A Valentine To Cherish
I Love You More
A Chocolate-Box Valentine
Valentine Hearts: 3 sweet and inspirational Valentine romances!

RECIPE FOR CHOCOLATE COVERED STRAWBERRIES

Ingredients:

1 pint (2 cups) fresh strawberries
1/2 cup semisweet good quality chocolate chips
1 teaspoon vegetable oil

Rinse strawberries and dry completely on paper towels. Line a cookie sheet with waxed paper.

In saucepan, melt chocolate chips and oil over low heat and stir frequently. Remove from heat.

Dip the lower half of each strawberry into chocolate mixture; and drip excess back into saucepan. Place on waxed paper-lined cookie sheet.

Refrigerate uncovered for thirty minutes. Store covered in refrigerator.

ACKNOWLEDGMENTS

An appreciative thank you to my patient husband, Dave, and our three wonderful children.

ABOUT THE AUTHOR

USA TODAY bestselling author, Josie Riviera, writes Historical, Inspirational, and Sweet Romances. She lives in the Charlotte, NC, area with her wonderfully supportive husband. They share their home with an adorable shih tzu, who constantly needs grooming, and live in an old house forever needing renovations.

To receive my Newsletter and your free sweet romance novella ebook as a thank you gift, sign up HERE.

You're invited to become a member of my Read and Review VIP Facebook group for exclusive give-aways, FREE ARC's, and much more!

josieriviera.com/
josieriviera@aol.com

ALSO BY JOSIE RIVIERA

Seeking Patience

Seeking Catherine (always Free!)

Seeking Fortune

Seeking Charity

Oh Danny Boy

I Love You More

A Snowy White Christmas

A Portuguese Christmas

Holiday Hearts Book Bundle Volume One

Holiday Hearts Book Bundle Volume Two

Holiday Hearts Book Bundle Volume Three

Candleglow and Mistletoe

Maeve (Perfect Match)

The Seeking Series

A Christmas To Cherish

A Love Song To Cherish

A Valentine To Cherish

Valentine Hearts Boxed Set

Romance Stories To Cherish

Aloha to Love

Sweet Peppermint Kisses

1-800-CUPID

1-800-CHRISTMAS

1-800-IRELAND

Irish Hearts Sweet Romance Bundle

The 1-800-Series Sweet Contemporary Romance Bundle

Holly's Gift

Seeking Rachel

A Chocolate-Box Valentine

A Chocolate-Box Christmas

A Chocolate-Box New Years

Leading Hearts

Chocolate-Box Hearts

Recipes from the Heart

A Chocolate-Box Summer Breeze

1-800-SUMMER

OH DANNY BOY (A SWEET CONTEMPORARY "IRISH" ROMANCE) PREVIEW

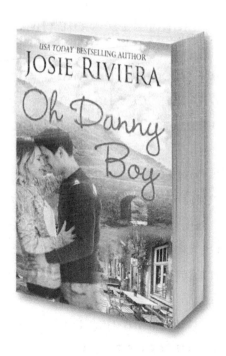

"Seamus, don't jump!" Clara Donovan heard her own

cries, the shouts resounding through the misty night air. She raced across the sidewalk toward Farthing Bridge, her gaze riveted on a horror she didn't want to believe. Her older brother Seamus sat on the edge of a tall bridge with his head slumped in his hands, a bottle of whiskey beside him. The arched stone bridge spanned the River Farthing, connecting the town to a once-popular marketplace.

No. It couldn't be. Her breath burned in her chest as she took in gulps of dampness and drizzle. *Don't stop. Run faster.*

When she reached the bridge, she elbowed through a group of late-night revelers. Several pointed up at Seamus. "He's off the rails!" someone shouted.

Her brother seemed unaware of the gathering crowd. He swung his legs back and forth like an underwound metronome and stared into the ice-cold river below.

She shook off the image of him on her living room floor several days earlier. He'd been passed out drunk. Should she have phoned a treatment center? No. She could fix her brother's problems. He simply needed encouragement, surrounded by his loving, supportive family.

Seamus. Gentle Seamus. Kind and fiery-haired, quick to temper, quicker to make amends. Her heart squeezed at the scruffy, dejected man he'd become since his wife had died.

Clara put her hands on her knees and took in calm, even breaths. Quickly, she assessed the corroded pedestrian catwalk leading to the top of the bridge, the skull and crossbones sign that warned *Danger*.

She stared upward at her sweet brother. "Dear saints in heaven, Seamus," she whispered. "You promised me that you'd never drink again."

She stuffed her wool gloves into her jacket pockets and bent to lace her weatherproof boots tighter. There was no time to dash around the river to the street that crossed the bridge, and she certainly wouldn't ask anyone in the crowd to lend a hand.

She yanked off the "Danger" sign and threw it to the ground. That pressing feeling in her chest, like she was running out of air, slowed her movements. Dragging in another breath, she grasped the slippery wet handrails and stepped onto the bottom rung of the catwalk.

"Missus, are you trained for this?" a man from the crowd inquired.

She glanced around. The man stood a hairsbreadth away. He was tall with piercing blue eyes and carried a guitar case. His dark brown hair had a reddish tinge and his navy wool jacket strained against his athletic form.

"Thanks. I can manage on my own."

Despite her refusal, she hesitated. Was she

trained to climb to the top of a rusted bridge when she was crippled with fear and could hardly breathe? Umm, no. But she was desperate, and desperation made people do things they thought they could never do.

"I insist." The man set his guitar case on the grass and stepped forward. "Who's sitting on the top of the bridge?"

"My brother!"

"I'll follow behind you. No worries."

No worries. Dear saints in heaven, her brother was about to jump off a bridge.

She gripped the slick railings with both hands and began climbing, acutely aware of the guitar player's encouraging whispers behind her. She counted each step until she reached the top, scrambled to her feet, and raced to her brother. Seamus's chin was hunkered in his hands, the empty whiskey bottle beside him.

She stopped a foot away from him. "Seamus, come with me."

His legs stopped swinging. He turned to her, his metallic-grey eyes glazed with drink. "What're you doing here?"

"I'm looking out for you, same as always." She attempted to keep her tone light. "The weather's a wee bit fierce up here. The wind and rain are driving my hair sideways."

Inwardly, she shuddered. He was a sight wearing

tattered clothes, his flaming red hair caught in a ponytail.

"And who's that dodgy bloke behind you?"

"Someone who's offered to help." She struggled to control her trembling. Her brother's big-boned body was precariously close to the edge.

Seamus's mouth twisted. "It's better if I end my life. I'm on me tod, I'm all alone."

She extended a hand. "You're not alone. I'm here for you."

Despite the chilly night air, Seamus was sweating. "I long for my wife. My beautiful woman ..."

"We all miss Fiona very much."

Seamus's fingers found the empty whiskey bottle and flung it into the river. "I'm warning you. Leave me alone or I'll jump." Slowly, he stretched out his hands.

"Seamus!" Clara hunched over, sick to her stomach, listening to the hoots and jeers of the spectators.

"Shut your gob!" Seamus hollered to the crowd. "Are ya' thick?"

Clara caught her breath. Stay calm. Level-headed and composed.

She straightened. "Those people won't help you, but I will."

What was she supposed to do now? Move slower, speak gentler? On watery knees, she started forward.

"You're managing perfectly," came the whisper behind her.

The guitarist. She'd almost forgotten. His breath was warm and reassuring against her hair.

She extended her hand again. "Please, Seamus, please. Come with me."

Seamus openly sobbed. "I'm no use to anyone."

"Think of Anna and me. We're your sisters and we love you." Clara tried to smile. "What would I do with myself if you weren't sleeping on my couch every night? You know I don't like to be alone."

Seamus squinted at her. Using his worn shirtsleeve, he wiped at the tear-stained bags under his eyes. "I lost all my money on the horse races. Five hundred euros that I'd borrowed from a friend, and one hundred euros of Anna's money, too. The bookies were certain Green Dragon would win the second race, but the ponies double-crossed me."

Clara dug her nails into her palms. "We'll pay the bookies all the money you lost." How, she had no idea. Her income as a factory worker and part-time dance teacher was scarcely enough to pay their current living expenses.

In the distance, insistent sirens blared, angry red lights flashed.

"Keep talking," the guitar player told her.

What to say? The wrong words might send her impulsive brother over the edge. She chanced a peek at the guitarist and lost her footing. Gasping, she held in a scream.

His arms went around her. "I've got you," he said softly.

She steadied herself and shook off his hold. Without making a sound, she ventured another two steps until she stood behind her brother. "We'll return to my flat and I'll light a fire in the hearth. Won't that be grand?" She heard her voice shake, the rale insistent.

"And make me a cuppa tea?" Seamus's copper-red beard showed days of neglect and grew in dirty spikes below his chin.

She placed her hands firmly on his shoulders and gave a reassuring squeeze. "I'll brew the entire pot and fry a proper Irish breakfast in the morning."

Several beats passed. Seamus seemed to be trying desperately to concentrate. He looked up at her. "You don't cook."

"I can manage fried eggs and bacon rashers."

He relaxed beneath her hands.

She licked her lips, her mouth so dry. "Please come home. Please. We're a family. We'll work this out together like we always do."

Seamus rubbed at his eyes, sniffled, and started to stand.

The guitarist stepped around Clara. Carefully, he assisted the wobbling Seamus to his feet.

The crowd applauded. They'd observed every de-tail of her family's private business. Clara pressed her lips tightly together, willing herself to think of her brother and nothing else.

Her sobbing brother slumped into her arms. She hugged him for a long time, then roughly shook his shoulders and stared into his bleary eyes. "I understand you're in a lot of pain. You'll be independent again, you'll see. It took me a long time, remember? And now I'm fine."

"Yeh." Seamus's lopsided grin showed missing teeth. He nodded so quickly that he stumbled, so unexpected they both cried out. She clung to his beefy hand, his body still so close to the edge of the bridge, as she stared into the frigid waters of the River Farthing far below.

"You'll both be safer away from the bridge." The guitarist's voice came loud and urgent. He guided Clara and Seamus to the side of the road, removed his jacket and placed it on the damp grass.

"Who are you, bloke?" Seamus asked.

"Danny Brady." He wheeled, clear in his intent to walk away.

"What about your jacket?" Clara called out.

Danny half turned and looked upward. The clouds had parted, the sky bathed in moonlight and stars. "No rain and no worries. Keep the jacket."

An emergency vehicle swerved onto the bridge, and Clara squinted into the blinding headlights. Several paramedics sprinted toward her and Seamus. A

Channel Four television news van streaked past, reversed, and screeched to a stop. A woman reporter and cameraman leapt from the van and scurried to the guitarist.

Clara recognized the reporter, Maeve Flanagan, an anchorwoman for the local television station. Maeve clutched the microphone, speaking urgently, then held the microphone out for Danny. He spoke lengthily, the bright camera light illuminating his china-blue eyes.

"Where are you from, Brady?" her brother shouted from across the road.

Danny's handsome face showed signs of fatigue. "Dublin." He focused on Clara. "Do you have a name, missus?"

"Clara Donovan." She nodded at her brother. "And this very foolish man is my brother Seamus."

From across the road, the reporter shouted, "May I quote you, Ms. Donovan?"

Clara stretched out a tired arm. "Absolutely not! And please take your slanderous reporting elsewhere!"

Maeve muffled the mouthpiece with her palm. In a loud voice, she asked, "Do I have permission to make a plea to the community on your behalf, Ms. Donovan? There are resources available for poor—"

Clara cut Maeve off with a wave. Heat flushed through her body. "My family fends for themselves,

Miss Flanagan! If you want to do something for us, then stay away!"

*** End of excerpt *Oh Danny Boy* by Josie Riviera

Copyright © 2018 Josie Riviera
***

Want more? Keep reading Oh Danny Boy on Amazon.

Free on Kindle Unlimited!

Made in the USA
Middletown, DE
20 September 2020

20239199R00099